The Journey of Two Broken Souls

CARLY BARONE

Acknowledgments

The love and constant support I have received throughout this journey as a new author has been amazing. I am beyond grateful to have achieved yet another success in life. I couldn't ask for better family and friends who believe in me.
To my family; Special thanks to my partner Raymond. You are my rock. You have been supportive of my writing journey from day one. You've motivated me to keep going when I get overwhelmed, and I cannot thank you enough. To my children, Rayianna, Gabriel, Raelle, and Noah, you four keep me on my toes at all times! You all are why I keep marching through life consistently, trying to be the best mother I can be to you. To my sisters Sabrina and Rachel, my mom Theresa, and my cousin Roxanne, thank you for putting up with so many phone calls and how-tos throughout my writing and publishing process. Thank you to my friends Adrienne and Kim. You all have been a blessing from God. I couldn't ask for better friends and family. I wouldn't have made it this far in my journey if it wasn't for all of you. You all have helped me so much to stay consistent and not give up, no matter how hard life hits me. Your support has not gone unnoticed.

From the ends of the earth, I cry to you for help when my heart is overwhelmed. Lead me to the towering rock of safety.

Psalms 61:2

1

Rose

On a cool day in September in New York City, a light breeze blew, and the sun shone brightly. A few other kids on the block and I ran up and down the street playing freeze tag. As we laughed and played, we all stopped when we heard a loud slam. Our eyes all moved to David. He was scary and hateful to anyone he came in contact with. Unfortunately, David also happened to be my dad.

We watched as my father stumbled down the stairs in front of our duplex and began talking loudly at no one in particular. I was only eight years old then and was embarrassed and ashamed of my dad. I only wanted to live a normal, happy life as any child would desire. Why couldn't I have that? I didn't think I'd ever know. My dad called out and instructed me to retrieve his keys inside our home.

When I returned, I placed them into his dry, callused hand and looked up at him. Hatred filled my father's eyes. I didn't understand why, so I turned around and ran back to the street, continuing to play with my friends. I could tell something wasn't right with my father. I had my suspicions, but what could I do at my age?

My dad was a hostile alcoholic who liked pushing my mom, Rebecca, around. Fortunately, for the most part, my dad would try to steer clear of me. Unfortunately, though, sometimes, if he were angry enough, he'd spank me also. I learned at a young age the difference between discipline and abuse. I had always told myself that I'd never treat my children the way my parents treated me.

I hated my dad as I grew older and began understanding what was happening. But I was too scared of him and wouldn't dare say how I felt. I had always thought he was disgusted by me, but I never knew why. So that afternoon, when I arrived home and walked through the front door, I planned on talking to my mother. When I walked inside, I found my dad intoxicated and passed out on the sofa. I shook my head and walked through the house, looking for my mother.

Once I found her in the bedroom, I sat on her bed. I expressed my feelings about how my father constantly mistreated her and me. I explained to my mom why I thought my father disliked me. After our conversation, my mother tried to comfort me the best way she could, only by bashing David. However, I still didn't quite comprehend the situation.

Six Months Later

Life didn't seem to get much better for me. It was either the same or worse. My mom used to be sweet and loving. She used to spend most of her time with me. I remember when we played tag and read books. She helped me with my homework and gave me tight, long hugs. I missed those days. But, due to David's abuse, Rebecca and I began to drift further apart. With my parents constantly fighting and the distance that grew between them, I knew something much more significant would happen soon. Something I still would likely not comprehend at my age.

Over the last three weeks, I'd wake up every morning to my father screaming at my mother. I've heard my father call my mother so many hateful names. I hoped no man would ever call me what my dad called my mom. But unfortunately, my father's daily drunken outbursts had become routine for me. So every morning at 6:15 A.M., I would hear my father screaming. It was like the most unpleasant, frightening alarm clock. The paper-thin walls in our two-bedroom duplex shook constantly, and the neighbors would always bang on the wall in their apartment. They could hear everything. The police had been called numerous times for noise complaints from our residence.

My dad would get so drunk that he didn't even care how loud and hateful he sounded. He continued throwing things at my mom. He kept yelling, slurring his words, and stumbling over himself. It really was embarrassing. Dreading what I was about to walk into, I rolled out of bed, opened my bedroom door, and looked down the hall. Ensuring I wouldn't be caught in the line of fire and take a chance of getting hit with a flying object as I made my way to the bathroom.

I made my way out of the bedroom, quietly tip-toed down the hall, and quickly closed the door. I brushed my teeth and washed my face. When I finished in the bathroom, I walked back to my bedroom and began getting dressed. I couldn't wait to get out of the house. I hated it here. After I got dressed, I walked out of my room and into my mother's room. I hugged her and then walked out of the house.

As I walked down my parents' duplex stairs, the boy next door walked outside and called out to me.

"Hey, tell your dad to shut up! You know, he doesn't have to wake up the entire neighborhood every morning."

I glanced over at the boy and then back down in embarrassment. My dad was indeed the talk of the neighborhood. I took a deep breath and thought about not going to school. Fearing all the kids would gossip about my dad being an alcoholic. I built up enough courage and walked to the bus stop. When I arrived, I heard some kids talking about my dad and me. Once the other kids noticed I was there, they all got quiet, and all eyes were on me. At this moment, I just wanted to run away and never look back.

Two Years Later

Things just continued to get worse for my family and me over time. I learned how to block out the noise from the constant fighting, my dad's drunken outbursts, and my mom's manic episodes. But I kept asking myself why. I couldn't understand why this was happening to me. Why couldn't I have a typical family that genuinely loved each other? Why couldn't my father see what he was doing to our family? Those same questions were repeated in my mind for a long time. Over the next few years, my mother became disconnected from life. I hadn't been getting the attention I desperately needed from my parents, especially my mother.

The following day, I woke up in a quiet house. Perplexed, I got out of bed, put on my slippers, and opened my bedroom door. I looked down the hall and saw no sign of movement. Grabbing my clothes, I walked to the bathroom, washed up, and dressed for the school day. When I finished, I gathered my belongings and heard my mother sobbing. I peeked around the corner into my parent's room and saw a suitcase full of my father's clothes packed neatly inside. This is perfect. He's leaving. I thought as I turned around and walked into the living room. I found my mother staring out the window, watching David fill the car with all his belongings.

Once David walked back inside the house, he looked at Rebecca disgusted and then at me.

"You see how you're acting in front of our daughter?"

Angry at my father's comment, I screamed.

"I hate you!"

I stormed out of the living room and back to my bedroom, slammed the door, and began crying. I stopped when I heard my mother begging my father to stay. I was confused and angry. I thought my mom would be happy if my dad left.

After that, I didn't want to call him my father anymore. It was just David. I truly believed that if David left, my relationship with my mother might get better and return to the way things used to be between us. I couldn't have been more wrong.

After David finished packing his belongings, he packed everything into his car. He then drove off, leaving my mom and me behind for good. I was ten years old when my father left. I felt numb, knowing that David's behavior had broken my heart and my family. Torn to pieces and thrown away like they were trash. I hated David for what he did to our family and for being unable to accept his only child.

Time passed, and my mother had changed so much that I didn't even recognize her anymore. My mother became highly depressed and hateful toward me. She told me that I was impossible for her father to accept. My being was too much for him to handle. I never expected that my mother's resentment toward my father would cause hatred toward me also after he left. So when Rebecca began treating me differently and blamed me for David's drug and alcohol addiction, I became defiant.

2

A week after my dad left, my mom hadn't gotten up from the couch except to go to the liquor store. Eventually, she began purchasing something more potent each time she went to the store. My mom needed something to keep her mind off the hurt David and I supposedly caused her. If I hadn't been so hard to love and care for, my mother wouldn't feel this way, and we'd all be together. After my mother gave birth and I came home from the hospital, David and Rebecca had been in love with me, but that was short-lived. I was very colicky when I was about three to six months old. Then, to make matters worse, I had been diagnosed with a ruptured eardrum on more than one occasion due to numerous ear infections.

We went through multiple surgeries before the doctors got everything under control. David couldn't handle my cries for more than a few minutes at a time, leaving all the pressure and stress on my mother, which in turn caused her to resent David. That was the main reason he began to drink, to start with, and things went downhill from there. I made my mother sick. She told me that if I didn't have all of those health issues, we would be a happy family, but instead, I had to come into our lives all messed up and then ruin her marriage. Not caring about my feelings, she told me she should have aborted me on several occasions. Sometimes I wondered why God allowed me to come into this world with the parents I had been given. It wasn't fair to any of us. From that day forward, I began to lose my faith in God.

Three Years Later

It was March twenty-fourth, my
thirteenth birthday. When I woke that morning,
I walked out of my room to find my mother in
the kitchen. Rebecca seemed in a good mood,
singing along to the music playing low.
However, as soon as Rebecca turned around and
looked at me, she exhaled hard.

"What are you looking at?"

Rebecca turned back around and continued to
make herself a sandwich. She scooped out some
mayonnaise to spread on her slice of bread and
put the jar back in the refrigerator.
I shook my head at my mother's ignorant
question and began to look through the cabinets

for something to eat and then closed the cabinet door.

> *"Is there any milk left?"*
> *"Milk for what?"*
> *"I thought I would have a bowl of* cereal."

Rebecca sighed, shook her head, and walked past me into the living room.
I tried avoiding any confrontation with my mother as much as possible. I hesitated to ask for anything else but worked up the courage to ask anyway.

> *"Since today is my birthday, could we do something together?"*

I desperately wanted to spend quality time with my mother but genuinely felt that I would never get it. I could tell by how my mom had acted towards me recently that she didn't care about spending time with me or that it was my birthday. It had been three years, and nothing had changed, but I still had faith and wanted to believe my mother would change and love me as she once did. A mother should love their child; I wasn't getting that from her.

I walked back to my bedroom and put on my clothes, shoes, and coat. Then I grabbed my book bag and headed out the front door for school. I walked all the way to the bus stop and then decided that I was going to skip that day. Since I've heard a lot of other kids do it, I thought I would too. So instead, I chose to go for a walk.

I walked down the street and through an alleyway before I got to the park. I saw some kids I'd seen from school hanging out by the pavilions. I began to wonder why they were all there so early. Then, I recognized two boys from school and someone else I didn't recognize. They stood with a man that looked much older. I walked over to the swings and sat down. I then pulled out my MP3 player and earbuds from the pocket of my book bag.

I sat on the swing for the entire day, just zoned out. I kept thinking about what I'd done wrong. I didn't understand why my mother hated me so much now. Finally, when 3 o'clock came around, I got off the swing, left the park, and walked home. Once I arrived and stepped inside, I snuck into the kitchen. I grabbed a few slices of bread and cheese and walked to my room. I closed the door, sat on my bed, and began writing in my diary.

The next few days, I decided to skip school again. I walked back to the park, sat on the swing, pulled out my MP3 player, and continued listening to music. I became suspicious when I kept seeing the boys from my school with that man. I watched them for about five minutes without making it obvious, and then I became lost in a song playing. Not paying attention to my surroundings, I looked up and realized that the same man was standing next to me. He had been trying to get my attention. So I took my earbuds out and looked at the man. He introduced himself and held out his hand to shake. His name was Jason.

Once Jason and I had become acquainted, Jason asked me why I wasn't in school. When I explained to him that my dad had left my mom and I was being mistreated at home by my mother, he looked shocked. I told him I couldn't concentrate on school and wasn't eating at home, so I went to the park to get my mind off things. At that moment, Jason convinced me to go with him to get something to eat. I told him I had no money, but he insisted on paying for my lunch. I then agreed and walked with him to his car.

When Jason and I pulled away from the park, he drove to Jimmy John's. Once we arrived, I explained to Jason that I had never been to Jimmy John's. Jason opened the door for me and allowed me to walk in first. We both took a few minutes to look over the menu. Then, Jason walked up to the counter when we both figured out what we would eat.

"I'll have a sixteen-inch ham and bacon and an eight-inch turkey. No mayo on either."

Jason paid for our meal and handed me my sandwich. Then, we walked over and sat in a booth. We began eating and getting to know each other better. Curious, I asked Jason how old he was, and when he replied 27, my jaw dropped, and my eyes widened—shocked at such a significant age difference. I then told Jason that I was only 13. Oddly, he didn't seem concerned one bit.

I began communicating with Jason more often after that day. Soon after, I fell head over heels for him. He was charming and gave me the attention I had longed for. Jason bought anything I had asked for, from food to new clothes, shoes, and even a cell phone so he could call me whenever he wanted. At thirteen, I was very naive and genuinely believed that Jason loved me. Why else would he spend all his time with me and money to buy me all those nice things? Not knowing Jason's ulterior motives, I was beside myself. I just wanted to be with Jason all the time.

My mom noticed that I was home a lot less than usual. Rebecca seemed not to care until she began receiving phone calls from the school resource officer. She was infuriated. My grades had dropped dramatically that semester, and I hadn't been at school in more than two weeks. A truancy officer was going to be sent to our house because of all my absences. Rebecca was threatened with jail time due to educational neglect if I didn't return to school immediately. I didn't really care what they did to her. In my mind, it wasn't only educational neglect that she should be worried about. So they just needed to lock her up and throw away the key.

One month into Jason and I's friendship, I built enough courage to ask Jason what he did for work. Jason sat back in his chair with a grin and lit a cigarette.

"I'm a pharmacist. I own the product, and I make my own hours."

I knew what Jason was getting at. I knew that he was selling drugs, but I didn't care. Sometimes you have to do what you have to do. I loved the attention and gifts, but I especially loved that Jason allowed me to ride with him all day.

"Can I work with you? I want to make my own money and work the hours I want. I can even help you if I go back to school. I could sell a lot there."

I tried convincing Jason to let me work with him, but he wasn't interested in hearing what I had to say. That evening Jason told me that he would take me home. I was distraught and refused to go back to my mother's house. I hated it there.

"You need to go home and see your mom. I'll pick you back up tomorrow, and you can ride around with me some more. Then, maybe we'll go out and get some new clothes. If

you're going to be working with me, you need an entirely new wardrobe."

Jason looked at me and what I was wearing and shook his head. I wore some faded, ripped jeans and a stretched-out t-shirt. I looked over at Jason from the passenger seat and rolled my eyes.

"Fine, but I won't deal with her attitude anymore. So, if she starts her mess again, I'm leaving. For good."
"You're not going anywhere. Do you understand me?!"

I jumped when Jason raised his voice. He had never yelled at me or so much as to speak in a higher tone. Still shocked and with a crackle in my voice, I asked,

"Why are you yelling at me?"
"Because you made me angry, Rose. Just stay here."

Jason pulled into Rebecca's driveway, stepped out of the car, and pulled my bags from the backseat. He followed me to the front door and handed me my bags. Rebecca opened the door as soon as I leaned in to kiss Jason.

"Where have you been?"

Rebecca looked at Jason, then back at me, and shot an awful glare.

"Get in this house, Rose. You've been skipping school, and now I'm being threatened about some resource officer taking me to jail because you won't do what you need to do!"

I walked through the front door and into the house. Rebecca looked at Jason, flipped her hair back, revealing her chest from her low-cut top, and smiled. She then closed the door, and Jason walked away.

Jason noticed the paraphernalia sitting in plain view on the coffee table. He knew the type of person Rebecca was, and he didn't mind one bit. Rebecca was the type that was going to spend money. Good money. It wouldn't be long before she found out who he was and where to find him for what she needed. Jason knew Rebecca wouldn't care that he and Rose were keeping company mainly because he would be her new main supplier. Win-win for everyone.

3

Rebecca had slowed up quite a bit on her drinking. Truthfully, I had rarely seen my mom drink anymore. But, unfortunately, Rebecca picked up on another not-so-good habit. She began buying pills, which then turned into heroin. I had become fed up with my mother and her drug use. She never had food in the refrigerator, the house was always a pigsty, and she had stopped paying the bills. All she was ever worried about was her dope.

I told myself that I'd be better off just going to school. I'd be able to get a free meal and a warm place to stay until Jason picked me up. So I dressed and walked out the door and to the bus stop. I was starving and couldn't wait until I arrived at school to eat. I wasn't too concerned about my schoolwork. My mother didn't seem to care much about anything but dope. So why should I care?

Jason had been much more distant lately. I was curious and wanted to know why. So as soon as Jason got there to pick me up after school, I planned on asking him what was going on.

So that afternoon, Jason pulled up to the school to pick me up. I opened the back door, put my backpack in the back seat, and jumped in the front seat.

"Hey, how was your day?"

"It was okay. I didn't do much. I had to run a few errands."

"Is there something going on? You've seemed a little distant lately. Am I doing okay with sales?"

"Yeah, but why are you questioning me?"

Jason got angry when I questioned him. He was not in a relationship with anyone, especially not a 13-year-old. I had heard him mumble.

Jason agreed to let me sell a few dime bags of weed at school here and there. He also told me how to sell to people discreetly. If I ever got caught, I'd need to run to the bathroom and flush my stash down the toilet. I did not want to have that on me if I got caught up. Not that my mom cared, but I knew I'd never have a chance to sell anything more significant for Jason in the future. It was too big of a risk. The heavier the product, the bigger the sale. They say money is the root of all evil, but I didn't realize how 'evil' the world could really be.

Wednesday morning came, and I went to school. Most of the kids were staring as soon as I walked into the building. One boy, in particular, stood out to me. It was the same boy from the park who was talking to Jason. His name was Alex. Oddly, Alex had shown a particular interest in me that day, and I wasn't sure why. I hadn't talked to him before that day. Alex was in the ninth grade and attended the high school next door to the middle school. I was a year behind him. I wasn't sure why he was hanging around the middle school, and I honestly didn't care until today.

I went straight to the girl's bathroom and sold some easy dime bags to a few classmates.

Afterward, I went to the cafeteria to get breakfast. When I finished eating, I went to my first class. I sold a few more dime bags throughout the day. It seemed easy. As long as I didn't get caught, I'd be fine.

After school, I gathered my belongings, stuffed my earnings into my backpack, and walked home. I always took a shortcut and cut through an alley and the park. Something odd in my gut told me to take another route, though. I decided to ignore the weird feeling I had and continued toward the alley. As I cut through someone's yard, I came to the alley and sensed someone was following me. Before I could turn around, Alex came out of nowhere and began talking to me. Then, he pulled me behind an abandoned house and pushed me down.

Alex attempted to force himself on me that afternoon. I resisted with all my strength, but he overpowered me. Alex pinned me to the ground and grabbed me by my neck. At that moment, I knew the only way out of this was to bite him as hard as possible. After I bit him, Alex screamed and picked up a brick. He then threw it at me, which caused me to lose my footing and fall back. He grabbed my backpack, took all the money I had made that week, and walked off. I got up, grabbed my things, and ran back to my mother's.

Once I arrived, I grabbed an ice pack and put it on my face. I hoped for the swelling from the knot I had to go down. I hoped it wasn't too noticeable, and then I looked in the mirror and saw the gaping gash on the right side of my face. *How am I going to hide this?* I thought to myself in a panic. I then remembered that all the money I had made was gone. Now I had to worry about Jason and wondered what he'd do to me next.

On Friday, I got up and dressed for school. After I left, Rebecca got up and left shortly after. While on the bus, I put on my headphones and looked out the window. It was almost an hour-long bus ride to school, so I sat back and tried to keep my face covered the best I could. Once my bus stopped at the railroad tracks a couple of blocks from my mom's house, I looked up and noticed my mother walking up to a silver car. Unfortunately, since the car's windows were tinted, I couldn't see who was in the driver's seat. Nevertheless, I watched as my mother and this unknown individual made an exchange. Then my mother walked back in the other direction.

I was furious. I knew what my mother was buying, but I was more curious about who she was buying from. I didn't know anyone with a silver sedan. A guy down the block sold weed, but Jason was the biggest dope dealer in the neighborhood, and he drove a white SUV. *Was there competition?* I wondered. When I saw him that afternoon, I was half tempted to bring it up to Jason. The only issue was that I had a massive bruise on my face and didn't have his money.

At the end of the school day, I pulled out my phone and checked to see if Jason had messaged me. I scrolled through my notifications, opened the text thread from Jason, and read the message that stated he was outside. I picked up my backpack and walked to the front entrance of my school. I looked around and didn't see Jason's SUV anywhere. I skimmed through the parking lot and noticed the same silver sedan I had seen earlier that morning.

Suspicious, I texted Jason back, asking where he was parked, and he replied immediately, in the silver car. My heart dropped.

Jason was now dealing to my mother, and I didn't want to believe it. Angrily, I walked to the car and got in. I pushed my backpack to the side and immediately turned to Jason.

"Are you selling to my mother?"

Jason, caught off guard by my question, replied,

"Why would you ask that?"
"While I was on the bus this morning, I saw my mother making a handoff with someone in this car. Was it you?"

Amused by my frustration, Jason laughed and then began to sweet-talk me. He explained that I should feel better knowing someone I could trust was dealing good product to my mom and not some half-cut crap someone just threw together quickly to make a few bucks.

It took some convincing from Jason to get me to come around. Finally, I gave in and let it go, understanding that it would be better if Jason dealt to my mother than anyone else. I didn't like that my mother had changed so much that she had now indulged in illegal substances. I still held animosity toward Rebecca because she mentally and emotionally abandoned me.

Rebecca didn't seem bothered with me or what I did, as long as she hadn't been dragged into it.

After Jason picked me up from school, he noticed the bruise on my face. He asked me what had happened. I was caught off guard and remembered that I had pulled my hood back when I questioned him about my mother. I told him I tripped and fell, walking up the stairs to my mom's duplex. Jason looked at me like he knew I was lying but didn't question me further. Instead, he turned his attention to the road, and we drove back to his house. Once we arrived, I walked into the house and sat on the couch. Jason asked for the money I made that week from sales. I took a deep breath, slowly grabbed my backpack, and pulled out a wad of cash. Jason took the money and immediately counted it. My eyes began to fill with tears, fearing what Jason would do to me if I didn't have all of his money.

"Where's the rest of my money, Rose? You were supposed to have $100."

"I was afraid to tell you. Please don't be mad at me."

"What are you talking about, Rose?"

I finally confessed to Jason about what happened to my face and the missing money. Last week I made remarkable sales, and word started to get around the school, so I had to slow up some and only sell to my regulars.

Jason was frustrated, knowing I couldn't have prevented what had happened. He sat forward, with his head in the palms of his hands, and thought about what to do.

"Who was it?"
"This guy Alex from the high school."

Jason stood up and walked into the kitchen. He stood beside me and held up a picture, questioning if it was the same Alex he knew and had working for him.

"Is this him?"

I turned around and looked at the picture, and nodded.

"Are you okay?" He asked me.

I looked into Jason's eyes and glanced down in shame. But then I saw the same thing in Jason's eyes that I saw in my father's eyes. Pure anger. Nervously, I took a step back, and Jason turned around and made a phone call.

Thirty minutes passed, and I was cuddled on the couch, still feeling nervous about what would happen after I lost Jason's money. Then, I jumped at the sound of a loud knock on the door. Jason opened the door, and Alex walked in.
Once Alex saw me, he smirked.

"What's up, Jason? I see you got a new piece."

Jason looked at Alex and then at me. He could tell how uneasy I felt, so he got straight to the point.

"You don't need to worry about her. But I need to know. Did you take money from Rose, Alex?"
"I don't know what you're talking about."

Alex looked at Jason and then at me. He began yelling at me and walking toward me. He called me a liar, and then Jason shoved him against the wall before Alex could say anything else. Jason clenched his hands around Alex's throat and began screaming at him. I was terrified and felt stuck.

Once Jason released his grip on Alex, I fled to the bathroom and locked the door. Jason began punching Alex; blood was all over the kitchen when he finally stopped. Jason walked out of the kitchen and tried to open the bathroom door. I panicked.

"Rose, it's Jason. Open the door. I need to get cleaned up."

I opened the door and stepped back. Jason walked in and motioned me to turn on the water. Once I did, I walked out of the bathroom and into the kitchen to find Alex half-dead on the floor.

When I witnessed Alex in that condition, I panicked and began hyperventilating. I had never seen that much blood before. I ran straight into the bedroom and cried. I felt relieved that Jason defended me, but I was terrified knowing that the boy who assaulted me was under the same roof as I was. After it was all said and done, Jason told me he loved me and would protect me no matter what. Since my mother abandoned me and David left, I had no one to look out for me. However, I cherished my friendship with Jason and fell for him even harder. I was afraid to leave Jason's side. I begged him to let me quit school and move in with him, but he had other plans.

A few weeks later, I noticed that Jason had been distant. He had been on his phone more often and hadn't been speaking to me much. So when he mentioned that he would take me back to my mother's the next day, I was heartbroken. I began to think he no longer loved or cared about me or my well-being by forcing me to return to my mother's. So that night, I decided to look through his phone when Jason went to sleep. I opened the text message threads and found a text from another girl Jason connected with. They had planned to spend time the next night, and my heart dropped.

I immediately got up and packed my bags. I didn't know where I would go or how I would get there, but I knew I wouldn't stay at Jason's or go back to my mother's. So I took a picture of the text thread. Then I sent the photo to Jason's phone, so he would get it when he woke up. I left Jason's house and walked down the street in the middle of the night. I was distraught and didn't know which way to go. Finally, I decided to go to the park. It was the only place where I felt peace. Once I arrived, I walked to a bench in a specific part of the park where I knew not too many people go. I sat down, put my backpack on one end of the bench, and lifted my hood on my jacket. I rested my head on my bag and fell asleep.

I was woken up some hours later by Jason standing over me at the park. It was four in the morning, and I remembered why I was there when I saw him. I immediately got up from the bench and tried to walk away from him. But when Jason pulled me back and into his arms, I cried.

"I thought you loved me. But I see you don't since you're talking to other girls. So why would you do this to me?"

"Rose, we are not together. We're friends. I said I love you because I care about you and don't want you to get hurt, but you're thirteen. So I cannot be in a relationship with you."

I begged and pleaded with Jason. I didn't care about the age gap between us. I loved him. Or so I thought I did. I tried convincing him to let me stay, but his mind was already made up. Jason tried to tell me that it would only be temporary and I could stay with him, but only sometimes. I didn't want to hear what he had to say and tried to walk away again. Jason grabbed my hand and told me he was taking me home, ending that conversation. I walked back to Jason's car and got in. We both sat in silence for the duration of the ride.

"I'll call you tomorrow."

I held back tears as Jason pulled into Rebecca's driveway. I looked at Jason, rolled my eyes, and got out of the car. I grabbed my bag from the backseat and slammed the door. Then, not saying a word, I walked into Rebecca's house and closed the door. I walked into my bedroom and sat on my bed. I pulled out my phone and pulled up Jason's number. I debated whether I wanted to block him or not. Finally, after about ten minutes of hesitation, I blocked his phone number, put my earbuds in my ears, and listened to music until I drifted off to sleep.

4

I hadn't spoken to Jason for a few days. I had no idea if he had tried to reach me since I blocked him when he took me home that day. I didn't care, either. I continued going to school, as usual, mainly just to eat. My grades had dropped horribly, and I couldn't concentrate on much of anything.

Monday morning came around, and I had to force myself to get up. I was running late and almost missed the bus. Once I finally got to school, I went to the cafeteria to get breakfast. I sat alone and ate, which wasn't uncommon because I had no friends. I had seen a new boy around school that day and wondered who he was. He was attractive, but my heart was still with Jason. Even after Jason forced me to go home so he could see another girl, I still cared for him. I was half-tempted to unblock Jason when I pulled out my phone to check the time. Then I realized that I had no service. I was confused as to why.

The last bell rang by the end of the day, and everyone was released. I walked out of the school's front entrance and noticed Jason's car parked in the parking lot. I tried to act like I didn't see him because I was still hurt by his actions last week. But I admit I was a little jealous. This was the first boy I'd ever loved.

I continued to walk toward the busses and had planned on getting on my bus. But, evidently, Jason had other plans and walked out between the buses to find me about to step onto my bus. He told me that he and I needed to have a conversation and I needed to go back to the car with him.

"Why do I have to go with you? Don't you have a new girl you're dealing with?"

He just looked at me and let out a small chuckle. Then he took my hand and led me toward his car.

Once we got in his car, he started the engine and looked at me.

"Give me your phone."

As soon as he said that, I knew where this was going. He hadn't been able to reach me since he dropped me off at my mother's house that night, and I blocked him. I knew he was more than likely mad because he was the one who bought my phone and consistently paid the bill. He took my phone and unblocked his number. Then he had the audacity to scold me like I was his child.

"You're not my father, so don't talk to me like you are!"

I shot back with a glare. I was fuming. Jason just looked at me and grinned. I didn't find anything humorous at all. I felt better afterward though because I felt like I stood up for myself for once in my life. I just didn't understand why he was so hateful. He said he wouldn't be with me because of my age, which made me wonder. *Why does it seem he is letting me keep the phone just to keep tabs on me? Why wouldn't he just take the phone and stop dealing with me entirely?* I didn't know what his intentions were. I wanted to believe that they were good and that he genuinely cared, but I couldn't tell what was real or fake about him at that very moment.

All I ever wanted was someone to care about me and love me the way I deserved to be loved. But I never knew what true love looked like because I'd never experienced it. So, I took any type of love and attention I could get. I knew I'd never get that from my parents. My dad was gone, and my mom was so doped up she didn't even think that trying to give me away as a payment to Jason would suffice for her habit. I was hysterical when my mother offered up that request to Jason. I knew what she was referring to, but I was thirteen, still very much a virgin, and wanted to keep it that way.

Even after my mother tried to use me for her habit, Jason never said a word about it after that happened. I was glad because I was terrified about when that day would come. I didn't know if it would be with Jason or someone else. But I hoped it would be Jason because I had fallen in love with him. I knew the age difference was still an issue, but maybe he'd come around after a while.

It had been four months since Jason and I had our disagreement after I blocked him. After that, I started to feel different about the situation between us. Our friendship seemed to get stronger over time. Oddly, since I defended myself, he had been acting differently toward me. He and I had gotten closer than ever before. I didn't know what had changed in him, but I liked it. I enjoyed our company even more than before.

I returned to Jason's house and got up to prepare for school. My fourteenth birthday was tomorrow, so Jason said he had plans to put some things together for me. When Jason dropped me off, he leaned in and kissed me passionately before I got out of the car. I was stunned—my first kiss, and with the man I loved. As my heart melted, I stepped out of the car and walked into the entrance of my school. My heart smiled, and I couldn't get Jason off my mind that day.

When school ended, I walked outside to see Jason sitting on the hood of his car, holding a bright pink gift bag and some roses. I was ecstatic. I ran over to him and jumped into his arms. I hugged him tightly, and he handed me a gift bag and roses. We got into the car, and I immediately opened the gift bag. I first found a card that was addressed to *'My Girl.'* When I opened it, it read;

"Roses for my Rose, thank you for staying loyal. Let's have some fun."

I continued searching through the gift bag, and as I pushed all the tissue paper to the side, I found a small silver box. I opened it carefully, revealing a gold chain with a rose pendant. I looked at him in disbelief. He smiled, said there was more, and motioned toward the gift bag. I continued ruffling through the tissue paper to discover five one-hundred-dollar bills.

Jason and I left the school parking lot and drove straight to get an early dinner. We ate at Baskin Robins and then ordered our desserts to go. I couldn't resist having a root beer float with extra whipped cream and cherries. Once we finished eating, we drove back home and watched movies for the rest of the night. Despite the gloomy and intermittent rain, Jason insisted on waiting for my birthday to go out and do something. The following morning, Jason woke me up and said,

"Good morning! Happy fourteenth!"

Jason had already been up long before me. I got out of bed and washed up, and dressed so we could go out to breakfast at Denny's. I devoured my meal expeditiously, but I noticed Jason was mostly on his phone while we were eating. I wasn't sure what he was doing or who he was talking to. I was tempted to ask but remembered the last time I questioned him. As he continued to finish his meal, I played a game on my phone until he was ready to go. I still felt put off knowing he had been on his phone most of the time we ate breakfast.

Once he finished, we both got up, then moved on to the next task for the day. While shopping, Jason played a big part in helping to choose what outfits I should get. We went to several outlet malls and bought several new outfits and shoes. I tried them all on, and he either approved or denied them. Then we moved on to choosing the shoes that I liked the most. Then, we went bowling and to the arcade to play games.—specifically air hockey and pool. I was surprised at how well I was at both of those games, not having played either of them ever.

Once finished at the arcade, Jason surprised me by taking me to a salon to get my hair and nails done. I had never been to a salon, so this experience was new and memorable. There was definitely something different about Jason and his behavior toward me. But it was different in a good way. At the salon, I got my hair washed, trimmed, and styled, and then I got a manicure and pedicure. While I was getting dolled up, Jason watched me the entire time. I felt a little awkward because he had a different look in his eye—A look I hadn't seen before.

When the stylists finished my hair and nails, I got up and looked at myself closely in the mirror. I looked beautiful. I looked a lot like my mother when she would do her hair and make-up. I began to think emotionally about her, knowing she hadn't called me for my birthday. Jason stood from his chair, walked over, and stood beside me. He turned to me, pulled out the necklace he had bought, and placed it around my neck. He reached down and hugged me from the side and whispered,

"You're my girl, now."

Hearing those words finally had me over the
moon. I couldn't be happier to be 'his girl.'

5

That night something definitely changed in Jason. It was like he had done a complete one-eighty. He didn't want to be in a relationship with me because of my age, but once I turned fourteen, he eventually called me his girl, and we were in a relationship. I wasn't sure what to make of it. Jason couldn't take his dreamy eyes off of me. After we left the salon, he made a comment that had me questioning him and me. He said after he leaned in and passionately kissed me,

"Are you ready to be with me?"

I wasn't sure exactly what those words meant. In my mind, I thought I was already with Jason. He then moved his hand to my upper thigh, and I eventually caught his drift. I just turned fourteen. I didn't think I was ready for intercourse. I expressed my concern to Jason, but his response was not what I had hoped. He explained that if I wanted to continue to be his girl, I'd have to push that fear to the back of my mind and go with the flow.

On the night of my fourteenth birthday, I lost my virginity. After it was all said and done, I began to feel very emotional. The entire experience was traumatizing. I wished I could've gone back in time and reversed everything that happened. I learned about sex in school and remembered that once you lose your virginity, it's gone forever. I wish I had heeded that warning. I told myself during class that day that I'd save myself for the right one and that God would honor the experience. I went to the bathroom and began having a silent emotional fit. I betrayed God and myself. I was too young to be having sex.

I didn't realize until about two months later that I had missed my time of the month. The possibility of pregnancy was not the first thing on my mind. In fact, it was the very last thing on my mind. I was still worried about knowing I'd never be a virgin again. If Jason and I had ever broken up, anyone else would see me as damaged goods. So I tucked the fear of pregnancy far back in my mind and assumed that I couldn't be because I thought it was almost impossible to get pregnant the first time anyone had sex.

The next few weeks were usual, other than my emotions getting the best of me. I had been attending class, doing surprisingly well, and receiving good grades in most of my classes. Finally, I walked to the cafeteria for lunch, picked up my food, and sat down to eat. I began thinking about the night of my birthday, and I truly believed Jason loved me. Why would he wait an entire year without expecting sex from me? That has to mean something, right?

After school, I decided to go back home to see my mother and pick up a few things from my room. As I walked into her house, it was dark and quiet. Not thinking of anything unusual, I continued to my bedroom to collect the few items I had left from the last time I was there. However, before I left the room, I noticed a folded piece of paper lying on my pillow with my name on it. It read:

> *"Rose, please forgive me for abandoning you. I have been selfish and did not do my job as your mother to put you first on my priority list. I sincerely apologize for all of the hurt I have caused you. I am signing myself into a rehabilitation clinic tomorrow to help me get clean. There are things that I need to confess to you, and I want to do right by you and be the mother you have always needed me to be. I hope you can forgive me. I love you, MOM.*

As I read my mother's letter, I began to cry. I left my room and walked through the house to find her. *Could she have left earlier than she said?* I thought. I continued to walk through the rest of the house until I found my mother lying face down on the bathroom floor, unresponsive. She had asphyxiated on her own vomit.

My body immediately went into shock after seeing my mother in the state that she was in. I couldn't move or talk. All I could do was cry. Soon it became difficult to breathe. Once I snapped out of the initial shock, I was afraid to touch my mother. I had never seen a corpse before and never expected to find my mother's. I took a step back into the hallway and immediately called 911. Then I texted Jason, who was sitting outside in the car.

Once he read my message, he ran through the door like a madman. I told him about the letter and how I found her in the bathroom.

"I called for an ambulance when I texted you."

"Wait, the cops are on their way here, now?"

I nodded, confused by Jason's question. He seemed rattled all of a sudden. I didn't understand why. Then, putting two and two together, I remembered that Jason was the largest dope dealer in the neighborhood. Now my mother was lying dead on her bathroom floor from an overdose of the drugs Jason sold her.

Jason, in a panic, explained that he had to leave before the cops arrived, with or without me. He wouldn't risk being questioned and taken into police custody. I tried fighting him, but he threatened to leave me and told me I'd end up in the foster system if I didn't go with him.

As soon as I heard the sirens, I panicked, grabbed my belongings, the note my mother left me, and ran out the door. I followed Jason to the car and jumped in, and he sped off. He took a few different detours before we arrived at this large house on the other side of town.

"Where are we?"

I asked as he directed me to get out of the car and follow him. We walked through the iron gate and down a long walkway to the house.

"Who's house is this?" I inquired.

Jason informed me that the house was his stash house. *I never pictured a stash house to be this charming.* I thought to myself as I walked inside and looked around. There was a strong odor that I didn't appreciate walking into, but the house was very nice.

"We're staying here for a while until things die down. I don't want to be out driving around too much with everything that's going on."

I could understand his concern, but I was still in shock after I had found my mother dead in her house. My mother and I had a lot of issues, and the abandonment I suffered was especially hard on me. Now knowing that my mother was dead, the feelings I had were unbearable for me to cope with.

Jason and I stayed at his stash house for a few more nights. By the following day, he thought it would be safe to go back home, and that's what we did. He switched cars again, and we left. As we drove through the neighborhood, we drove by my mother's duplex and saw the bright yellow caution tape on the door. I began sobbing when visions replayed in my mind of my mother's lifeless body lying in a puddle of her vomit. I had nightmares for weeks after that. I wouldn't wish death on my own worst enemy. I wish I had been there earlier to find her before anything happened. No matter how upset I was, I wished I had the chance to forgive her for what we had been through.

After everything I had just been through and witnessed, I was distraught. The entire situation seemed not to affect Jason whatsoever. I didn't understand him. When Jason found out I had been sexually assaulted, he came to my rescue immediately after I told him what had happened. But now, my mother had more than likely passed away from the drugs Jason had dealt her. Yet, he seemed not one bit bothered, and that bothered me. This was my mother, and it felt like she was just another dollar sign to him. Ever since then, I have looked at him differently. I couldn't even look at him without getting upset.

I hadn't gone to school for a few days. I also hadn't told anyone about my mother's death either. So when I walked through the school doors and then into the cafeteria, everyone turned to look at me. As I walked through the line to get my breakfast tray, a few people approached me to give me their condolences. How did they hear about my mother? I had no clue. After breakfast, I stood up, threw my trash away, and walked to my first class.

A light, nauseous spell came over me as I walked down the hallway. I didn't think anything of it and continued to class. I walked into class and sat down. I began to copy the notes that were written on the board. Suddenly, my mouth began to salivate intensely, and I became nauseous again. I jumped out of my seat, covering my mouth as I ran to the bathroom. I violently threw up everything I had just eaten that morning.

The sight of vomit seemed to throw me into a traumatic spell. I fell back into the wall and screamed. I began breathing so fast that I started hyperventilating and couldn't catch my breath. Before I knew it, I fainted right there in the bathroom stall. When I came to, two teachers, the vice principal, and the paramedics stood over me. I was loaded onto a stretcher and wheeled out of school and to the hospital.

When the ambulance arrived at the hospital, they took me straight to a room in the emergency department. The nurses came in to assess me, and the doctor walked in and put some orders in for lab draws. After an hour of waiting for the results, the doctor finally came back in to talk to me. She told me my blood pressure was low, I was dehydrated, and I had a urinary tract infection. That didn't seem too serious, right? Wrong! The doctor then told me that they also ran a pregnancy test when they ran my urine sample. To my surprise, I was eleven weeks pregnant, and my due date was December twenty-second. To make matters worse, my unborn child's father was my drug dealer boyfriend who killed my mother.

6

When I had been released from the hospital, I called Jason to tell him what had happened. I told him what hospital I was at and asked that he pick me up. Once he arrived, I got into the car and drove back to his house. I got out of the car, walked inside, went straight into the bedroom, and got into bed. I fell asleep almost instantly and slept until my alarm clock alerted me to get up the following morning.

I got out of bed and went straight to the bathroom. I felt like I had to pee every five minutes. Jason asked me why I was going to the bathroom so often. I explained that when I went to the hospital, they told me that I had a UTI, which was the cause of my fainting. Also, I had been dehydrated, which also played another part in urinating so often. I was eleven weeks pregnant and hadn't shared the news with Jason yet. I didn't want to tell anyone. But I knew I had to tell Jason, but I didn't know when. So I decided to drop the bomb on him on the way to school.

I got dressed, and then we walked out the door. I was still angry with Jason for disregarding my feelings when I lost my mother. But I didn't feel it would be right not to tell him that he had a child on the way. I didn't know how I would break the news to him, so I just blurted out,

"I'm pregnant."

He slammed on the brakes as he backed out of the driveway and looked at me. He didn't look happy or sad. It was hard for me to read his body language.

"So you're just going to spring this on me suddenly and think I'll be cool with it?"

The way Jason asked me that made me think he didn't want the baby. When the truth finally came out, I was heartbroken.

"Rose, I don't want any kids. So, if you're thinking about keeping that one, think again."
"What are you saying, Jason?"
"I'm saying I don't want a kid. So you need to take care of it. I'll give you the money to get rid of it."

That day was my breaking point. I snatched off the necklace around my neck that he had gotten me for my birthday. I threw it at him and said,

"Oh, the same way you got rid of my mother?!"

Then, I got out of the car and ran. The words *get rid of it* kept replaying in my mind. I couldn't believe him. I ran in the direction of my school until I couldn't run anymore. I was afraid that all this stress would cause me to lose my baby. Maybe that was Jason's goal now, to keep me stressed out and pick unnecessary fights with me so I'd have a miscarriage. But I wouldn't allow it. I knew I didn't want to return to his house after what he said. So I continued to walk to school and would hopefully come up with a plan by the end of the day.

Once I arrived at school, I saw two police cars parked in the front. I debated whether I should have gone to school or hung out elsewhere. Until I had the urge to urinate, I would have a big accident if I didn't find a restroom fast. I walked into the front office, hoping to run by quickly so no one saw me, but as soon as I opened the door, the front desk receptionist stood up and said,

"Here she is, Officers."

I stopped and looked at both of the officers and asked,

"Can this wait? I have to use the restroom now."

I quickly ran to the bathroom and then tried to collect my thoughts before I walked out to see what this was about. Considering the circumstances, I had a feeling it was about my mother. As I left the restroom, I passed the new boy I'd seen not long ago. I continued through the office and walked up to both of the officers that were waiting for me. They began speaking to me, but it was like I had tunnel vision and couldn't hear what they said. That was until a woman from children and family services stepped in.

My heart dropped when I remembered what Jason had said after I found my mother. I followed the officers, Janice from Children and Family Services, and the principal into the principal's office. The officer shared the news about my mother and that they had been searching for me. They asked where I was and if I knew what had happened to my mother. I tried to act like I didn't know, but one of the officers told me about another letter they had found that my mother had written. The letter explained that my mother had failed me and turned to drugs and alcohol after my father left. My mother said in the letter that I had been in a relationship with an older man. That man had also been the one who had been supplying her with drugs.

Now that the truth was out, I had no choice but to explain my version of events to the police, and the reason I ran was because I was afraid. I also confessed about my pregnancy and was worried that any more stress could potentially cause harm to my unborn child. The adults were all shocked to hear this. I asked what would be done to Jason. Janice put her hand on my shoulder, and in a soft tone, she explained that the State of New York would more than likely press charges against Jason for statutory rape. He would also likely have been charged with narcotics distribution and drug-induced homicide. But, it would be up to the prosecuting attorney. I then asked what would happen to my unborn child and me. Janice said they don't usually have good outcomes for cases like mine. However, it'd be a miracle if they could find a foster family or an adoptive family willing to take on the responsibility of my child and me. She whispered that the state might convince me to abort my pregnancy. But Janice made it a point to say that if I were sure I wanted to keep my unborn child, she'd fight tooth and nail for that to happen.

Janice reassured me that she would put me down as a top priority. I wasn't sure how to take that. Why wouldn't I be a top priority? Janice then requested my schoolwork from the principal for the next two weeks. As we waited patiently in the office for them to bring my schoolwork out, Janice continued asking me questions. Finally, a short time later, my principal walked into the office with a manilla envelope. I took all my work, and the two police officers escorted her and me to her car in the parking lot.

Janice asked if I'd seen an obstetrician for my pregnancy. I told her I hadn't seen anyone other than the doctor in the emergency room when I fainted. Janice explained,

"Now that you're a ward of the State of New York, we're responsible for you and your health. So I'll schedule your prenatal appointments to ensure everything goes well throughout your pregnancy."

I'm glad she was on board and wanted to ensure the baby and I continued to stay healthy. I agreed and then inquired about how soon I should be seen and if Jason would have any rights to my child after I deliver. Janice had an idea of how uncomfortable I was if Jason were to get custody of my child after it was born.

"Since charges are more than likely to be pressed against Jason, I'm not sure he will have rights to the baby if he is found guilty of those charges. But I won't say that will definitely happen. If Jason beats the charges, there is the possibility that he could potentially fight the state for custody which wouldn't look good for him. If I were you, I would try to put that to the far back of your mind for now."

I could tell by Janice's demeanor that she tried to alleviate my concern and did a good job.

It had been two weeks since I had been taken in as a ward of the State. Eight weeks into my pregnancy, the morning sickness was horrifying. I had an appointment to see the doctor to get checked out and ensure the baby and I was healthy and doing well. I'd get an ultrasound at my next appointment to see the baby, and I couldn't wait to see my bundle of joy on the ultrasound monitor. Unfortunately, Janice still hadn't found a suitable foster home for me. I had been living in a group home, and truthfully, I thought living with my mother was bad. This place had rats and leaks in the roof, and the food was disgusting.

I was half-tempted to run away. I didn't know how much longer I could live in a place like this. I had no friends, and most kids placed there were strung out on something. They required me to do group counseling services. I had to attend but refused to talk about anything I had been through. I felt uncomfortable because most of the girls there would gossip about me because of my pregnancy. The boys just looked at me like I was an easy piece of meat. So, I didn't want to put all my business out there to a group of other kids I didn't know.

I contemplated a way out on more than one occasion. But, once I had an open window of time, I worked up the nerve to make a run for it. As soon as I was about to slip out, the head lady of the house called down to me. I opened the door to the office of the group home, and the woman told me I had a phone call. I walked over and picked up the receiver that sat on her desk. It was Janice.

She thought she had found a foster home that would take me in. It was a bittersweet moment. I was overjoyed because I might get to leave this place, but my mind began wondering. I was afraid if the group home I was in was so awful, what would the next place look like? I didn't know if I'd be sent to another group home or if I'd be sent to live with foster parents that I knew nothing about, and they didn't know me either. Janice explained during our call that I would need to only stay in the home for another month so she could tie up some loose ends with paperwork if it all went through. Then I could finally pack my belongings, and she'd pick me up from the group home.

Once I hung up the phone, I ran out of the office and headed back to my room. I was ecstatic. I ran down the hallway and right into Kristian. Shocked after what had happened, I looked up at Kristian, who was also stunned by the run-in. He stood there perplexed, but with a soft smile, he held out his hand to help me off the floor. I grabbed hold of his hand, and he pulled me up. I couldn't help but look at his beautiful light brown eyes. From that point on, I was mesmerized.

7

Two Months Later
Kristian

Ⅰt was a Friday morning, and I was supposed to go to school, but I begged to stay home. I had been having a lot of trouble lately with nightmares. Two years ago, I was placed in the foster system. I wouldn't say I had a terrible life, but it certainly wasn't something I'd be proud to admit. I never got hurt physically, but what I saw, mentally and emotionally, ruined me for a long time.

I remember my mother telling me she named me Kristian because I am a man of God. I grew up in church, and I attended youth group often. I watched my father struggle with demons for a long time. He fought the urges and tried getting counseling and attending church as often as they had service, but it didn't work. It ruined him in every way.

Unfortunately, on my twelfth birthday, I watched my father pull out his gun, shoot my mother, and then turn it on himself. I remember, before hearing the second gunshot, he turned to me and said, *I'm Sorry*. Since that day, I have struggled with nightmares, depression, and anxiety. The flashbacks of seeing my mother lying dead and then my father soon after had me mentally and emotionally scarred. Sometimes I would question God and wonder why something like this would happen to my parents. They were good people. They struggled in different areas of their lives but loved and cared for one another. Loving and serving God the only way they knew how. Things just became too much for them to handle.

Once the police came, they took me in for questioning. After answering their questions, I was released into the state's custody. Since then, I began to defy anyone who took authority over me, including God. Throughout this entire situation, I lost my parents, my home, my friends, and even my faith. I had no one to turn to. I was thrown into the system like a was a piece of trash. I blamed God for everything that happened.

I was officially in the state's custody for four years when I turned sixteen. No one even wanted to be bothered with me. I was in and out of foster homes. No one was willing to take on a teenage child with severe mental and emotional challenges, specifically concerns like mine. I had been placed back in the group home, and I began to doubt everything until one day, I walked into my room and found a note on my nightstand. It read,

'Kristian, Follower of Christ.'

At that moment, I panicked. I remembered how my mother used to tell me that before she died. I wasn't sure where this came from or who wrote it, but I would not let it go until I found out who it was and why.

I ran out of the room, into the TV room, and then into the office. When I saw Janice, whom I was highly fond of because she seemed to be the only one who genuinely cared about me in that place. I ran into the office and pleaded to Janice that she tell me who left that note on my nightstand. When Janice hung up the phone, she looked at me, smiled, and pulled out my file from her desk. She handed me a piece of paper that stated my birthdate, my name, and the words *follower of Christ.*

"This was found in a box in your mother's closet. The box was retrieved from the house once you were taken into state custody. But I'm glad you came to see me about it because I wanted to be the first to tell you that I decided to open a community center for struggling youth. I won't be working here anymore."

I wasn't sure how to take that. Janice was the only person who looked out for me and ensured I had everything I needed. I didn't know what I would do when she left.

"What's going to happen to me if you're leaving? I won't have anyone."

I tried to hide my emotions, but I realized over the years when I attempted to hide those feelings, I would lash out. Janice was the only person who could talk to me about my feelings and get me to fully open up about it, but now she was leaving.

"Well, Kristian, come into the meeting room with me so we can talk more."

I was perplexed by her comment and unsure how to take it. Then, still trying to contain my emotions, I began feeling apprehensive as we walked into the meeting room.

Once we walked into the meeting room, I found another woman sitting at the table. She looked back and forth through my file and a stack of papers on the table. I sat down at the oblong table and looked at Janice,

"Kristian, this is Olivia. She works with the state also, and she'd be taking my place here. She had a question for you."

I pulled out a chair, sat at the table, and looked at Janice and Olivia. I still needed to understand. But, not wanting to plant false hope, being the reason another state worker was in the meeting room with me. It was overwhelming. Olivia stood up from the table, smiled, and held out her hand to shake. She introduced herself and then asked me if I had the option to be adopted by Janice, would I be interested in carrying on with the meeting? I knew Janice, and I trusted her. I hesitated initially, wondering if I had heard Olivia correctly, so I asked for clarification.

Once Olivia confirmed my suspicion, I couldn't contain my emotions. I immediately jumped out of my seat, ecstatic that Janice was willing to adopt me. I didn't know what would happen to me if she left, and I would have to get to know someone new. I had difficulty opening up to Janice when I first got brought into the group home. Now, she's the only one I could openly talk to without feeling uncomfortable. I was thrilled about starting a new life with my adopted mother.

A month later, I was in a courtroom facing a judge with Janice and Olivia by my side. On Tuesday, June eighteenth, I was no longer a ward of the state. I had been adopted by my case worker. The same woman who had taken me into the state's custody when I lost my biological parents. I was back in church consistently, began making friends, and my life was great. But something was missing. I wanted to do more with my life—something better. I explained how I felt to Janice and told her I wanted to become more involved and help around the group home.

Once I explained that I wanted to give back to the group home and the state for allowing Janice to adopt me, she contacted Olivia. When Olivia got word of my request, she was proud to offer me to go back to the group home to volunteer. I helped around the office, took out the trash, and talked to some of the other kids still there awaiting adoption and foster homes. That's when Rose and I collided in the hallway. I couldn't have been more grateful for that encounter.

Rose turned out to be a beautiful soul. I knew she was pregnant. It was kind of hard not to figure out when she was running to a bathroom or trash can every five or ten minutes throwing up. If I'm going to be honest, it made my job more complicated because I did take on the task of cleaning up the group home and taking out the trash to help out around there. Some of the boys there would ask me how I felt cleaning up vomit all day long. It really didn't bother me. After seeing my parent's brain matter splattered on the wall of my house, bodily contents didn't bother me much anymore.

I felt for Rose because she was brought into this world by parents who didn't care for her how they should have. Rose searched for love and attention in all the wrong places, and she found it in a much older guy who got her pregnant and then told her to abort it after he found out. I couldn't imagine feeling her heartbreak. Knowing that she gave some guy her body and her heart, and this is what she got in return. Rose doesn't know, but she's stronger than any other girl I've known. She's pregnant, in the foster system, and fought to keep her unborn child. That alone says a lot about her character. If only she hadn't been hurt so much and was willing to open up, she could realize who genuinely cared for her.

I truly wanted her to find a home with parents who cared about her and wanted what was best for her and her child. The only problem was that few people wanted to adopt a teenager, much less a pregnant one. That night after Janice and I went home, I lay in bed thinking of how we could help Rose and get her out of there. I didn't want her to stay there until she had that baby. Neither Rose nor her baby deserved to grow up in a group home. I began thinking of everyone Janice knew. At that moment, a thought crossed my mind from a conversation I had overheard when Janice and I went to church last weekend.

I jumped out of bed and walked into the living room to find Janice sitting on the couch, eating popcorn and watching a movie. I sat next to her and said,

"I have a confession, but I feel like this is what God would want me to do. So I wanted to talk to you about something."

Janice looked at me with suspicion. Still trying to figure out where I was going with this, she sat up, muted the television, and gave me her full attention. I cleared my throat and started talking.

"When we were at church on Sunday, I overheard you talking with Sarah and Pastor Robert. You all talked about how they had difficulty getting pregnant, and Sarah desperately wanted a family. So my request to you is that you would consider talking to them about Rose. I'm worried about her and don't

want her to have the baby while still in the system. I should be a perfect example of how hard it is to grow up in the foster system. I know this is probably completely out of line on my part, but will you please just talk to them for me?

Janice's eyes filled with tears at the thoughtfulness of my request, and she agreed to talk to the Pastor and his wife. There was definitely something about Rose. I couldn't seem to get her off of my mind. *Was it love? If that was the case, I was all for it. I felt that God wanted our paths to cross for a reason. I wanted to be her knight in shining armor. I wanted to be with her, be the best for her, and I'd fight to make that happen. But how do I know if she likes me the way I liked her? Would she even want to give me the time of day if our friendship could be taken to the next step?* A lot of questions were thrown around in my mind. I began to self-doubt my feelings and became anxious. I kept my feelings to myself and hoped and prayed things worked out how I pictured.

8

Rose

When I ran into Kristian in the hallway, my heart fluttered. It was an odd feeling. One I hadn't felt before. I tried to figure out what it was about him. It was a feeling of peace. I'd never had that feeling with Jason. I felt safe with Kristian. There was a connection from the moment we laid eyes on each other at school. But this time was different.

My run-in with Kristian was completely unintentional. I ran so fast down the hallway that I practically barreled right through him. I was just as stunned as he was. I was slightly embarrassed because I fell when our bodies collided. The way he immediately helped me off the floor and asked if I was okay was heartfelt. The genuineness that he showed was like I'd never experienced before. I wasn't sure how to perceive it.

Over the course of a month or so, Kristian and I had become close friends. I liked him a lot, but I allowed my fear to get the better of me. I refused to allow myself to open up to him too much. I wasn't sure if he viewed me the same way everyone else at the group home did. I never disclosed my pregnancy to him. I didn't know if he knew, but I wasn't ready for that disappointment if he decided he didn't want to associate himself with me. Mainly because my morning sickness had worsened by the day. I knew I couldn't hide it much longer as my belly grew.

Another week went by, and Kristian and I began communicating even more. I found myself opening up little by little to him. We shared our experiences living in the group home and how we came to stay there. I was hesitant, but the way he was so patient with me and my feelings made me feel comfortable with him. I felt so ashamed when the question was finally

asked how far along into my pregnancy I was. I
wished I was invisible.

Kristian immediately began to console
me and then, to my surprise, reassured me. He
explained that he knew that I was pregnant
when I first arrived, and he didn't feel that I was
any of those things the other kids said about me.
I felt such relief when he expressed his thoughts
about my situation. Knowing that he was such a
genuine and supportive friend melted my heart.
I couldn't have asked for a better friend.

I began coming out of my shell more
often since meeting Kristian. I was overjoyed to
have people like him and Janice in my corner. I
obviously made some mistakes in life and got
into a situation with someone I thought was my
friend and boyfriend. Now that I'm pregnant,
that would be an impossible situation to get out
of. It was most definitely a learning experience,
but I knew I had two solid supporters to guide
me down the right path. I struggled with my
emotions and had to navigate life as a pregnant
teenager living in the foster system. After I lost
my mother, I still had nightmares pretty
regularly. I'd see her lifeless body lying on the
floor and have a panic attack again. I had to find
my way. It took time, and I struggled for a long

time. Thankfully, Kristian and Janice were there for me through it all.

I was now four months pregnant. My belly had just started to show, and it was almost impossible to hide unless I wore an oversized t-shirt. Kristian finally admitted to knowing about my pregnancy and wasn't judgemental or condemning. Instead, he reassured me that he wouldn't leave my side and would help me as much as I would allow. He admitted he was falling for me, and he was unsure of my feelings. That was why it took him so long to admit it. Kristian also explained that I would have to open up to him for him to help me when I needed someone to be there for me mentally and emotionally.

It was August, and I had horrible hot flashes from the pregnancy. I was scheduled to see the doctor to determine the gender of my baby in a couple of weeks. I walked into the office and sat in the chair, attempting to rest my feet. The pressure from the extra weight I was carrying started to cause swelling in my feet, and I was sore. I didn't want to lay in bed because it hurt too bad from the springs popping out of the mattress.

I received a phone call from Olivia, who wanted to meet the next day to discuss potential options for me if I was interested. The next day when I met with Olivia in the meeting room, I found Janice and Kristian also sitting at the table with Olivia. I asked what was going on, and then I was made aware that Kristian had requested that Janice and Olivia have a meeting to talk with me about my placement and what Kristian had on his mind regarding potential adoptive parents. When Olivia and Janice explained everything in detail to see how I felt, I looked at Kristian with pained eyes. Then, without saying a word, I stood up and stormed out of the office and into the bathroom across the hall.

Janice walked into the bathroom shortly after to see if I was okay. Violently, I vomited as tears flowed out of my eyes. I felt betrayed by Kristian because he didn't come to me first to tell me about this plan he had for *my life*. How did he think I would be okay with his plan? But, of course, it could've been the hormones talking because the thought of it after the fact didn't sound so bad. Janice and I talked for a little longer in the bathroom, and then we walked back into the meeting room where Kristian and Olivia were still sitting.

Embarrassed, I asked that I had a moment with Kristian to talk to him about what happened. I noticed how Kristian immediately stood up, walked over to me, and put his hand on my shoulder. He looked into my eyes and told me that I didn't have to apologize for feeling upset about it. He also claimed he could've handled the situation a little better. He admitted instead of blindsiding me and not making me aware of the topic of the meeting, he could've and should've talked to me beforehand. I appreciated him for his thoughtfulness. I couldn't be more grateful for someone who genuinely had my and my baby's best interest at heart.

I agreed to return to the meeting room with Kristian to discuss the potential adopters. As we walked into the room, Kristian stood up, pulled out a chair, and I sat beside him. I listened carefully to every piece of information they gave me about the potential adopters and their life stories. They sounded like a really lovely couple who just had an unfortunate chain of events happen. With Sarah unable to conceive naturally and not wanting to use medications and surgical procedures to force herself to get pregnant, Kristian came up with the idea of adopting my unborn child and me.

"Are they willing to really adopt the baby and me?"

I asked openly as they all looked at me, willing to answer any questions I may have had. Janice mentioned,

"I brought it up in conversation if they were given the opportunity to adopt, would they be willing to adopt a young girl who's expecting? I didn't want to give them too much more information than that until we got an answer from you."
" I would like to meet them. But, I won't say I will go through with the adoption process off the top because it's not only about me anymore. I have a child to think about too."

I explained my concerns and requested that I meet the potential adopters. Truthfully, both Sarah and Robert sounded like good people. Kristian told me Robert was the pastor at his and Janice's church, and Sarah was his loving wife. I didn't feel like Kristian or Janice would steer me in the wrong direction when it came to my life and safety. After all, they were the only two that I could genuinely trust. So I decided to go through with the meet and greet with Sarah and Robert to see how things went— it was the second-best decision I've ever made.

Janice and Olivia took the necessary steps to set up a meeting with the Johnsons. I was nervous, but I knew this needed to happen. I was getting closer to my due date and wanted to be in a home with loving adoptive parents when I brought my child into the world. So I would do whatever I needed to allow this to work out. Looking back on my life, I was terrified for my child. From that day on, I promised myself that I'd do anything to make sure that my child never went without, whether it be physically, mentally, or emotionally.

It was September eighth, and Janice and I were on our way to my ultrasound appointment. Naturally, I was anxious to find out the gender of my little bundle of joy. Once we walked into the doctor's office and signed in, I sat patiently, waiting to be called back. While waiting, Janice leaned in, told me Kristian had texted her and wished me luck. I couldn't help but smile. I also couldn't help but fall more in love with him. The only problem was I was afraid to tell him how I felt because I didn't know how the conversation would go and if he even wanted to be in a relationship with me the way I desired.

Lost in my thoughts, I didn't even realize that Olivia was standing next to me, nudging me to get up because the nurse was waiting for me to go back for my ultrasound. I stood up quickly and followed Olivia and the ultrasound technician to the back. When I entered the room, it was dark, and a blanket was lying on the bed. The technician asked me to remove everything from my waist down to prevent getting gel on my clothing and place the blanket over me, and she'd be back soon.

I did as I was instructed and sat waiting on the bed. When the woman returned to the room, she grabbed a pair of gloves from the box on the wall and sat down in her chair. She began asking me questions to verify who I was and then started the ultrasound. It took about twenty-five minutes, and then I knew it was time to find out what I was having when she asked if I wanted to know the gender. Happily, I nodded and closely watched the screen on the ultrasound monitor. I was amazed that I was carrying a life inside of me, and when she finally got to the correct position, she wrote *'I'm a Girl!'* on the screen.

I was beyond excited and blessed. I couldn't have been happier. As soon as I was finished, Olivia and I left the doctor's office and went straight to get lunch. During that time, I requested to use her phone to call Janice and Kristian to let them know the news. So I dialed Janice's number and waited for her to answer. To my surprise, a handsome-sounding voice came across on the other end.

When Kristian answered the phone, I heard Janice in the background asking what the ultrasound results said.

"It's a girl!"

I yelled into the phone. I then heard Janice in the background shouting excitedly. Finally, Kristian softly spoke into the phone,

"Congratulations. You're going to be a great mother, Rose."

Hearing those words caused my heart to swell. The feelings of joy and love came over me. I decided that when I got back to the group home with Olivia, I would talk to Kristian about how I felt about him.

Once Olivia and I arrived at the group home, we walked inside and into the office and noticed it was silent throughout the building. Olivia and I put our bags down and walked down the hall to see where everyone had gone. When I opened the door to the lunch room, everyone was whispering and stopped and stared when they saw me. I was the center of attention, and I hated it. I left the room and went to lie down for a while. I felt upset because I could never escape the gossip around me. I was the talk of the neighborhood when my mom and dad split and at the group home too. I couldn't catch a break.

9

It had been three weeks since I discovered I was having a girl. I had a notepad and a pen with me everywhere I went, jotting down names of what I may name her. I would think to myself how I was really a mother. It was a scary feeling knowing that I was carrying a baby and going to be raising this child for the rest of our lives.

I had yet to see Kristian around lately. I wasn't sure what to think. I wondered if I should contact Janice to get ahold of him. But I thought he might not want to talk to me anymore. I didn't want to seem needy, but I wanted to speak to him about how I felt. So, I reached out to

Janice anyway and asked where Kristian was. When Janice told me Kristian had gotten a job and had been working a lot, I thought I'd never get the chance to talk to him.

It was September twenty-eighth, and I had a meeting with the Johnsons. Of course, I was nervous about meeting them. I didn't have a clue about these people at all. But I trusted Janice and Kristian that they would do right by my baby girl and me. So I walked into the meeting room with a clear head and my notebook to ask any questions I may have thought of. At the meeting table sat Janice, Olivia, and Kristian. I was upset that he had just decided to show up to the meeting after being MIA for weeks.

When Mr. and Mrs. Johnson arrived at the meeting, I instantly felt a shift in the atmosphere. There was a feeling in my gut that I'd not had before. Sarah held herself high and confident, with a loving disposition. Robert was laid back, humorous, and carried the same confidence and loving personality as his wife. They were eager to get to know me and about my pregnancy. Sarah was thrilled when I revealed that I would be having a girl. She asked me if I had any names picked out that I would like to name my daughter. I explained I had a list of names I wanted to choose from. Eventually, I decided on the name Veronica. Sarah and Robert both loved my choice of a name for my daughter.

Robert asked if I would feel comfortable sharing my life story with them. I was initially hesitant, but I felt peace over me instantly. I began to explain the chain of events that had taken place since I was a child. When I finished explaining everything, I noticed Sarah coming to tears. My life wasn't easy, and there were many things I constantly struggled with, but with consistent love and support, I could get through it. Robert was very empathetic. But when he asked me about my likes, dislikes, fears, and dreams, I wasn't sure how to respond. I never thought about it. In reality, I never had the chance.

Three hours in and we finally came to an agreement, and the meeting came to a close. I was happy to say that Pastor Robert and his wife Sarah were moved by my story and wanted to take on the responsibility of being my and my daughter's adoptive parents. So, out of habit, I extended my hand to shake, and Sarah and Robert pulled me in for a hug.

The feeling I had when around Sarah and Robert was like nothing I'd ever experienced. I had to thank Kristian for coming up with such a thoughtful idea. Since I met him, he had been nothing but good to me. It was like he was my guardian angel. I couldn't have been more grateful for all the people I had in my corner.

On October sixteenth, Olivia requested a court date to push the adoption through sooner because my due date was approaching fast. I was seven months pregnant, and these beds in the group home started to feel more like barbed wire cots. The cushion seemed to have diminished, and I was constantly aching. I began panicking because we were running out of time, and I still needed to go shopping for the baby.

I called Janice to contact my adoptive parents to see if they would be willing to allow me to set up a baby registry while I was still at the group home waiting for the court date. Once I explained that I was getting scared because I didn't think we would have time to prepare for everything we needed to do for the baby and my arrival, Sarah and Janice were already working on a plan of their own that I knew nothing about.

When I got permission from Sarah, I contacted Kristian and asked him to help me work the computers at the group home. They were old and outdated, and most needed a software update. Kristian had always been tech-savvy and knew much more than I ever did. So he set up a computer for me, and Janice came in to help me find baby furniture and necessities to add to the registry. I picked out the crib, swing, bottles, diapers, and chose some different clothing options.

About three weeks later, Olivia came to me with the good news that the court date was scheduled for November fifth. That would give me three days to pack up my belongings and get ready to move in with Sarah and Robert. I took my time folding the little clothes that I had, which were entirely maternity clothes. I was moving slowly because I was so sore. My entire body ached, and I hated every minute of my third trimester. I wanted this pregnancy to be over so I could hold my little girl. I was in the nesting stage of my pregnancy and cleaning up anything I could.

Once November fifth came, I got prepared for the day in court. Olivia drove me to court and stuck by my side the entire time.

She knew I felt nervous, but she talked me through the process before we went in. Finally, at 9 A.M., I went before a judge with Sarah, Robert, and Olivia by my side and Janice and Kristian behind me. I remembered hearing the gavel slam against the judge's wood desk after he heard the information from all parties involved, and I knew I would go home with Sarah and Robert afterward. I felt beyond relieved.

When we left court, Sarah, Robert, and I went out to eat for a celebratory dinner. Olivia, Janice, and Kristian drove off in the opposite direction. Once we arrived at the restaurant, we were seated and began ordering our food soon after. After we finished our meals, we drove back to Sarah and Robert's house. This was the first time that I had been to their house. It was a stunning four-bedroom, three-bathroom home with a large fenced-in backyard in a nice neighborhood. From what Sarah explained, the school districts were excellent. When we walked through the front door, we were greeted by Janice, Kristian, and Olivia. The house was decorated with pink balloons and streamers. Gifts were spread out on a table in the corner, and a baby shower cake was on the counter.

"You all did all of this for me?"

I asked, surprised. I couldn't believe all the trouble they went through to make this day memorable for me.

Sarah wrapped her arms around me and motioned me to follow her and Robert through the house. She wanted to show me where everything was and the rooms they had decorated for the baby and me. As I entered the first bedroom, Sarah explained it was my room. There was a beautiful red oak bedroom set with a large dresser full of clothes, a chest of drawers full of infant clothes and other necessities, a bassinet, and an infant swing. In addition, the room had a large walk-in closet with shoes and more clothes.

As we walked out of my bedroom, Robert took me to the bedroom directly across the hall and opened the door. He allowed me to step inside, and I instantly burst into tears. The purple and pink walls immediately told me this was Veronica's room. When I walked into the room, a giant picture of Veronica's name was painted on the wall. Her room held a full-size crib with a changing table on one side, a chest of drawers with a picture of my first ultrasound image that I was given, a rocking chair, and an abundance of diapers, wipes, and anything that Veronica would need.

Once we finished the walk-through, we walked back into the living room and gathered around the table. I received cards and more gifts, and then Kristian handed me a box wrapped neatly. I unwrapped the present from Kristian, which revealed a brand-new iPhone 12. Kristian explained that I hadn't seen him often because he had gotten a new job, and he wanted to work to pay for my phone, so he and I could communicate more often. I leaned in, hugged him tightly, and thanked him. Sarah immediately said the phone service was already activated and I would be on their family plan. So whenever I needed to get a hold of anyone, I would always have a way.

As everyone gathered, ate cake, laughed, and spent the rest of the night together, I looked around and realized something. My life spiraled down at a young age, but I was blessed to have such loving friends and adoptive parents to support me. I initially lost hope, only to realize that God was there the entire time and had a plan for my life. I knew I had a long road to recovery after losing my parents, Jason, and coping with my pregnancy. I gained hope back and pushed forward to give Veronica and me the best possible life.

10

Things had gotten much better for me
as the weeks went by. Sarah and Robert were a
true Godsend. We all woke up the following
morning, and Sarah immediately put on a pot of
coffee for Robert and her. Robert stood in front
of the stove, piling food on plates as we sat for
breakfast. Not only was Robert a pastor at our
church, but he was also a fantastic cook. He sat
a dish filled with eggs, bacon, biscuits and
gravy, and blueberry pancakes with a glass of
orange juice in front of me. I loved blueberry
pancakes.

I remember how my mother made them for me when I was young. It was nice to keep those good memories alive, but knowing how life played out and that she was gone now hurt. The flashbacks of seeing my mother still haunted me, but they didn't come as often as they used to. I was grateful for that. Sarah and I talked a lot about grieving and the seven stages that are commonly talked about. I was stuck in the fourth stage of grief, depression, reflection, and loneliness.

I thanked God every day for allowing Kristian to cross my path. I might have never met Sarah and Robert if it wasn't for him. Kristian had been a tremendous support throughout my grieving process. He knew what it was like to experience losing a parent, but he lost both of them, and the incident occurred in front of him. Kristian and I spoke every day. We helped each other heal from our past and leaned on one another when things got hard.

A few days passed, and Kristian came by to spend time with me. We spoke for hours and then decided to take a walk through the neighborhood. Suddenly, Kristian stopped walking and turned to me,

"Rose, would you like to go on a date with me?"

I was speechless. Something I had been waiting for, for so long, and I couldn't even say anything. As I tried to collect my thoughts and figure out how to say yes without sounding overly excited, Kristian looked at me blankly and sighed. I felt horrible. I didn't want to lose my only chance and cause him to feel bad, so I shouted,

"Yes! I'd love to go on a date with you. I thought you'd never ask."

Immediately, Kristian looked into my eyes and grinned. Then, he reached out, locked his fingers with mine, and continued walking.

It was Christmas Eve, and Kristian and I were on our fourth date. He and Janice showed up at my house, dressed casually, walked inside, and waited for me patiently in the family room. Sarah helped me get ready and kneeled down to zip up my boots because my belly had gotten in the way of reaching my feet.

"I can't wait to see my feet again, much less reach them."

Sarah giggled at my comment, and Janice then opened the door to sneak inside to look me over. She hugged me and tucked my hair behind my ear.

When I was ready, Sarah, Janice, and I walked into the family room to find Robert and Kristian debating who would be going to the Superbowl in February. I giggled as they argued about who was the best team. Eventually, Sarah blurted out loudly to get the guy's attention and let Kristian know I was ready to leave for our date.

Kristian, Janice, and I walked out the front door and got in the car. Kristian insisted on taking me downtown for a horse and carriage ride through a sea of Christmas lights for our date. I had never been on a carriage ride, and it seemed romantic. I loved that he put so much thought into our date night for us. It meant a lot. Kristian expressed how special I was to him, and he thanked God for me every day.

Once we arrived downtown at the booth to pick up the tickets Kristian had purchased online, we walked over to the carriage to wait for the man to prepare the horses for our ride. When the horses were ready, Kristian helped me into the carriage first and climbed in after I was seated. He sat next to me, handed me a blanket to cover with, and wrapped his arm around me. It was twenty-eight degrees, and it started to snow as the ride began. The view of the chain of lights while on the carriage ride was breathtaking.

The carriage ride lasted almost an hour. We were given mugs of hot chocolate to enjoy on the ride, and as we came to the end of the ride, I began feeling pains in my lower stomach. I didn't think anything of it when the pain started. I initially thought Veronica was moving around and things were fine. Unfortunately, the pain got worse throughout the ride, and I didn't realize that I was squeezing Kristian's hand every time the pain got worse.

"Hey, are you okay?"

Kristian asked, concerned when he watched my other hand hold my stomach.

"It's probably just these seats. They're a little uncomfortable to sit on."

I told Kristian that I thought it was the seats to not cause him to worry, but in my head, I was panicking.

The pain I was experiencing wasn't like any other pain I'd felt throughout my pregnancy. When the carriage ride ended, Kristian got down and held his hand for me. Once both of my feet hit the ground, I took two steps, and then I felt an enormous amount of pressure and heard a splash.

"Kristian, please don't panic, but I think my water just broke."

I suffered excruciating pain in a split second and let out a horrifying scream. Kristian immediately pulled his phone from his pocket and called Janice. As soon as she answered the phone, Kristian yelled into the phone,

"Rose's water broke!"

Janice told him to call Sarah and Robert and have them meet us at the hospital. Janice had been parked close by, so she could get to us

quickly to provide help and head for the
hospital.

When we arrived at the hospital, Kristian
ran inside to notify the front desk to come out
and help me. There was a group of nurses and
doctors huddled around Janice's car. They
loaded me on a stretcher and brought me
straight into the hospital. I was taken up to the
labor and delivery floor and admitted. The
doctor on call came into the room quickly and
spoke to me while the nurses attached heart
monitors around my stomach. The doctor
checked my cervix, told me I was six
centimeters dilated, and explained that I would
have my daughter on Christmas Eve.
        Shortly after, Sarah and Robert arrived at
the hospital. I requested that only Sarah and
Janice be in the room with me during delivery.
Having the guys in the room while my legs
were up and my female parts displayed for
everyone to see felt awkward. Gladly, the men
agreed and happily got comfortable in the
waiting room. Unfortunately, I was dilating so
quickly that I couldn't be given an epidural.
        As my labor progressed, the doctor came
in about twenty minutes later to recheck my

cervix. I had dilated to nine centimeters and would soon begin to push. I didn't know the pain would be so bad, which caused me to have an anxiety attack. I started hyperventilating, and I couldn't get it under control. Janice and Sarah, both standing on each side of the bed, tried to console me to allow me to slow my breathing, but it didn't work. The monitors began blaring, and several people ran into the room. Before I knew it, I fainted.

When I woke, I was surrounded by family and friends in a different room. But what I needed to understand was what happened and where Veronica was.

"What happened?" I asked no one specifically.

Once everyone in the room heard my voice, Robert immediately called for the doctor, and they all huddled around my bed. Sarah explained that I fainted and it took time to get Veronica out. There was some concern that Veronica lost blood flow, and I had to have an emergency cesarean section. Veronica was placed in an incubator with high oxygen flow to help her breathe. I felt horrible. When I panicked, I put stress on Veronica and caused this all to happen. I felt guilty, thinking that if something more significant was wrong with my baby, it was my fault because I panicked.

Kristian walked over and placed his hand on top of mine. He told me that anxiety during such an event was expected and that I should not beat myself up about it. Then, he reached out his hands and requested that Robert pray over Veronica and me. Everyone stood there while Robert prayed over us. I felt a change in my body. Peace took over my mind and body, and the anxiety left instantly. The doctor came in and looked over me and told me how I gave everyone a good scare. I nodded and asked about Veronica and how she was doing.

The neonatal nurse entered the room at that moment, pushing a cart holding Veronica. I leaned forward in bed and looked through the plastic box covering her. She was still on oxygen because she couldn't breathe well yet on her own. The nurse allowed me to hold Veronica as long as she had a face mask attached to the oxygen tank to continue getting air. As the nurse carefully picked up Veronica and handed her off to me, I fell in love with my daughter all over again. Janice asked me what her middle name was going to be.

"Veronica Serenity Johnson. Veronica means she who brings victory, and Serenity means peaceful."

I was proud to think of such a powerful name for my daughter. She was tiny, but like me, she was a fighter. She weighed six pounds and ten ounces and was nineteen inches long.

Veronica was in the hospital for two weeks before her lungs were strong enough to breathe on her own without the assistance of the oxygen. She was seen by a neurologist before we were cleared to go home. We were told that Veronica may show mild developmental delays due to her oxygen being cut off while I was in surgery for the cesarean section. After being discharged, I had a list of follow-up appointments for her and me. I still beat myself up about throwing myself into a panic. It caused me a lot of unnecessary stress and put my daughter through a lot. I tried to stay hopeful that things would improve over time, but I began suffering from post-partum depression.

It had been two months since Veronica and I had been home. Veronica had been doing well, and we hadn't had any trouble with her breathing. She was quiet and rarely cried. When she did, it was only when she wanted to be changed or fed. I, on the other hand, was a complete mess. I became distraught over the slightest mishaps. I was exhausted and cried myself to sleep nearly every night. I tried to figure out what was wrong but couldn't control my emotions.

The following day Sarah came into my room, and we talked about how I had been feeling. She explained that it sounded like I was suffering from post-partum depression.

"Sometimes, after a woman has a child, they can experience post-partum depression. It is common and doesn't mean anything is wrong with you. But, after having the baby, sometimes your body and hormones have a hard time getting back to normal. So maybe it's a good time to get you into the doctor to get checked out to see if you're experiencing a hormone imbalance or if it could be something else.

I agreed with her. I didn't want to continue having these issues. It made it harder to take care of Veronica, and it caused a strain on my and Kristian's relationship.

It took around two months to get my emotions and hormones under control. I often spoke with Sarah, Janice, and Kristian to help me cope with my feelings, which helped tremendously. I could even go on dates again with Kristian while Sarah kept Veronica at home. That helped Kristian and my relationship to grow much stronger. Knowing that he understood everything that took place and how to help me through it made a world of difference.

11

Since Veronica had been home, she had improved her breathing. In addition, she's progressed toward her developmental milestones and did much better overall. Things were finally back on track with my hormones, and I had been doing much better with coping skills. Sarah and Robert explained that now that Veronica and I were doing better, it was time for me to be enrolled back into school. Due to the concerns about attending school in person full-time, Kristian presented the idea of enrolling in the private school associated with our church.

Robert and I agreed with Kristian's suggestion and contacted the director of New Life Academy and explained the situation. He and Sarah were able to work out a deal with the school that I attend full-time, taking online courses four days a week and physically participating in class one day a week. Sarah agreed to make that work to stay home with Veronica while I was at school, and I could stay home with her the rest of the week. But there were stipulations. If I couldn't keep my grades up, I'd be required to attend at least four days a week. I knew this would make it hard for Sarah to work if she had to watch Veronica while I attended school. So I agreed with my parents and the school that I would work hard to keep my grades up.

On my first day of school, I was nervous. Not about going to a new school because I barely knew anyone at my last school, but because that was the first time I'd be away from Veronica for an extended time. I was afraid to leave her side. Robert and I stepped out of the car and walked into the front office. Robert already knew the principal because that was the school associated with the church he had pastored at. We walked inside so I could meet and talk with the principal. I had to physically attend my classes that day, so I could get my schedule, formally meet my teachers and pick up my books.

After I met the principal, I grabbed my schedule from the secretary and hugged my dad. Then, I walked to my first class, and before I walked inside, I texted my mom to check on Veronica. She instantly replied with a picture of my baby girl holding her bottle. I was excited for her, but I felt guilty at the same time. By being at school, I thought about how many milestones Veronica would hit while I was gone. My mom texted me back and wished me good luck on my first day. That helped me to begin the school day with ease.

I breezed through the school day with no issues. I had extra time to finish any homework I had been assigned so I could go home and spend time with Veronica. When the bell rang, I packed my bags and walked to the office to pick up my Chromebook to sign in from home for the rest of the week to do my schoolwork. I was given all the sign-in information to log into the computer and my school account. I was happy they were willing to work with me, so I could stay home, still care for Veronica, and attend school. I found Sarah in the parking lot waiting for me when I walked outside. I ran to the car excitedly because I knew she had brought Veronica. I placed my bags in the front seat and hopped into the car's back seat with Veronica. I leaned over and gently kissed her cheek, amazed at her beauty.

Once we arrived home, Kristian and Janice waited for us in the front yard. We got out of the car, and I grabbed my bags. Kristian ran to the other side, unbuckled Veronica, and toted her car seat inside. At the same time, I followed behind him with all of my bags. In the house, we sat down to talk, and Veronica started crying. My mom had to leave for a few hours to work at the church, so Janice and Kristian stayed home with me to help me with Veronica and get my computer and internet equipment set up for tomorrow. Janice jumped up to tend to Veronica, and Kristian walked me through the setup process for the computer and internet.

After Kristian and I hooked up the computer to the hotspot, we took Veronica for a walk around the neighborhood. Janice stayed behind at the house to do light cleaning in Veronica's room since mom had to leave suddenly to help my dad at church. It was nice having such loving and supportive friends and family. During the walk, I noticed how close Kristian and Veronica had become. Their bond was unbreakable, and Veronica loved him. So did I, but I didn't think we were at that point in our relationship to verbalize it to each other.

On our way home, Kristian expressed how he wished he lived closer. However, he loved being around Veronica and me. He mentioned how he would be looking for a car so he could drive over every day. He reached out his hand, locked his fingers in mine, and kissed the back of my hand. I knew God placed Kristian in my life for a reason. He was nothing like Jason. Kristian was genuine and pure. He'd never raised his voice at me. Anytime he disagreed with something I did, he politely explained what he thought I could've done differently. Kristian was helpful and encouraged me to keep studying hard in school. He expressed how proud he was of me. He asked if I'd ever be interested in being a trauma counselor for teens like us who grew up in the foster system. I told him it sounded like a great idea, but I'd have to get through my last year of middle school and then high school.

Kristian explained that he would be willing to stay home with Veronica so I could take some extra courses to graduate early. If I attended summer school also, I'd also have additional credits to graduate earlier. He was willing to do whatever was necessary to help Veronica and me improve. I always wondered what his intentions were. *Did he expect to get something from me in return?* I thought. I wanted to ask him, but I didn't want to offend him by asking something like that. He's never requested anything like that from me, so I was trying to figure out what to think.

My mind was overthinking, and I wanted it to stop. I know overthinking could cause harm to a relationship, and I didn't want to be the cause of that harm for thinking a way that I should not.

Veronica was now eight months old, and she had been doing great. The doctors in the hospital before I brought Veronica home told me that she may never meet all her developmental milestones. But, by the time she was six months old, she was right on track. Things at school had been going well, and I'd been staying on track with my studies.

The following day, I had to be at school early to prepare for a presentation due. Kristian dropped me off, and as I walked across the street, I noticed someone who looked very familiar to me. I couldn't figure out who it was or how I knew them until I heard a voice that called out my name and sent chills down my spine. I remembered that voice all too well from my childhood. My dad was back.

I looked at David across the parking lot, and he approached me. I told him I wasn't interested in speaking to him and that we had nothing to discuss. As I continued to walk into the gate of the schoolyard, David yelled out again,

"I have vital information for you; you will want to hear it."

I kept walking, trying not to listen to him, but what he said was horrifying.

"It's about Jason."

Hearing Jason's name made me stop in my tracks. I was trying to decide whether I wanted to run or see what he had to say. I turned around and yelled back to him,

"Give me a minute to put my things down, and I'll be back out."

David nodded, and I walked inside the office and placed my bags next to the secretary's desk. Then, I walked outside to see what craziness would come from David's mouth this time.

I walked up to David, and he said he had a message to relay from Jason.

"How do you know Jason?"
"He and I were in jail together until he got transferred upstate. He told me to let you know he was getting out and wants to talk to you."

The sound of Jason's name made me nauseous.

"Yeah, well, did he tell you why he was in jail, to begin with?"
"Yes, he did. I'm sorry about your mother, by the way. He also told me I have a grandchild."

"Don't you dare bring my child in this. You or Jason will never see my daughter! I'm done with this conversation and am going back to school now. Have a great life."

I turned around and began to walk away until I heard David say,

"He's getting out of jail, Rose. He called me last week."

I immediately went into panic mode. I walked into the office door and pulled out my phone. I put Sarah and Janice on for a conference call and explained the events outside my school. I told them not to let Veronica out of sight and to come to the school and bring her with them. I had a very unsettling feeling in my gut. As I sat in the office waiting for my parents and Janice to arrive, I tried to cope with my anxious feelings.

Once my parents and Janice arrived at the school, I ran outside, grabbed Veronica, and carried her inside. My dad requested that the principal allow us to use his office to discuss some things. After we all stepped into the room, I explained again what had happened with

David and what he had told me about Jason. Then I looked at Janice and asked what she knew about Jason's release.

"I thought he wasn't getting out, Janice."

Janice called Olivia and relayed the message. She put the phone on speaker, and Olivia began looking up information on her computer.

"I see here that Jason beat the charges due to insufficient evidence. Clearly, someone at the police department dropped the ball because if he gets out or gets moved, his case gets flagged, and we're supposed to be notified immediately. It states that his release date was March twenty-fourth."

"It's May. So was he released already?"

When I heard that Jason was released on my birthday, it brought back memories. Memories that I shouldn't have been thinking about. But I'd never have Veronica if it wasn't for that day.

Two weeks had passed since I saw David at my school, and I was distraught over the situation. Since I learned about Jason's release, I have thought about him a lot. It caused a lot of stress on me when I thought about my mother and how Jason was the cause of her death. In addition, there had been a strain on Kristian and my relationship, and we weren't doing well either. I had become distant toward everyone and felt like my life was in shambles again. If David knew where I attended school, it would only be a matter of time before Jason showed his face. But I didn't expect him to show up at my front door.

12

I had Veronica in the bathtub when I heard a knock at the door. Kristian came over a few hours earlier to help with the baby, so I could work on an essay due soon. I finished earlier than expected and had some time to wash up Veronica before she went down for her afternoon nap. Kristian answered the door, and I could hear another man's voice. The next thing I knew, Kristian walked into the bathroom with a troubled expression.

"What's wrong?"

I asked. I began to worry because I had never seen Kristian without a smile on his face.

"There's some guy on your porch asking for you."

My heart dropped when he told me that. I already knew it was Jason. But I didn't know how he found out where I lived. I never told Kristian about the message that David relayed to me about Jason. I felt the need to keep that to myself. So Kristian probably thought I was seeing someone behind his back, which probably caused him to have that look on his face.

Kristian stepped in to take the baby and finished rinsing her off. I got up and walked outside to find Jason standing on the porch. I kept telling myself to keep my distance, but as soon as I closed the door behind me, Jason leaned in and hugged me. Caught off guard, I stepped back and unwrapped his arms from around me.

"What are you doing here?"
"I hadn't seen you in a while and wanted to know how you were doing."

There was a silent pause for a few seconds, and I could hear Veronica crying inside the house. Jason looked up at me and said,

"So I take it you kept the baby?"

"Jason, we have nothing to talk about. I have to get back in there. Please don't come back here again. If you don't leave now, I'm calling the police."

Kristian stepped in the doorway as I opened the door to walk inside.

"Is everything okay, Rose?"

Jason laughed and looked Kristian over.

"Who is this? Your bodyguard?"

Fumes were erupting inside me, and I became angry. I walked inside, pulled Kristian back, and closed the door.

I was livid. After everything Jason put me through, he had the audacity to show up at my parent's house. What was he trying to do to me? I asked myself. I had to have this conversation with Kristian and explain what happened from the beginning so he could understand. I had no desire to be with Jason. He may have been my daughter's father, but I did not want anything to do with him.

It took some time to explain to Kristian that Jason was a thing of the past and he also was Veronica's father. I told him I refused to go backward and was happy with my life. I was comfortable in my relationship with Kristian. Later I spoke with Janice and Sarah about Jason showing up at the house. I still didn't know how he found out where I lived, and with Veronica, I felt unsafe. I expressed my concerns to my parents, and we thought getting an order of protection against him would be a good idea.

I asked Janice if I would have any problems with Jason trying to file for custody of Veronica. She explained that not only because of his charges, and now that Veronica and I had been adopted, Jason had no rights to her. Janice put my mind at ease with my concern. She also spoke with Kristian about what had happened in an attempt to ease his mind as well. Surprisingly, I discovered that Kristian had a completely different view on things than I did.

Kristian came by to discuss Jason's visit a few days later. He sat down with Veronica and me and explained why he had a different outlook on the situation. Kristian told me that even under the circumstances and after everything I had gone through with Jason, I'd need to follow God's word. This meant I would have to allow myself to forgive Jason for what he had done to me. I stared at him in disbelief. I wasn't sure if I heard him clearly.
Utterly shocked, I wasn't sure how to perceive his instruction.

"Kristian, that man took advantage of me. Yes, I was naive and didn't know any better because I didn't have a proper role model to look up to. He had me selling drugs for him, and I allowed it when I found out he was selling them to my mother. That is how my mother died. She asphyxiated on her own vomit, overdosing on the drugs he gave her! Then he convinced me that he'd care for me, got me pregnant, and told me to get an abortion! How am I to forgive him for that?

Kristian didn't show a single crease on his face when I explained how I felt. Instead, he nodded and agreed with me. Validating my feelings. I was perplexed because he seemed to show he cared about how I felt, but he didn't seem to get off the subject of forgiving Jason. I didn't know what I could say to make him understand that I couldn't forgive Jason though.

"Rose, please don't take this the wrong way. I care for your well-being mentally and emotionally, and I also care about your and Veronica's safety. You may feel like you cannot forgive him now, but with time and support, you'll come to a point where you will feel it's only right to forgive those who've wronged us. It could take a week, or it may be years. Just think of Veronica. Don't put that burden on her because of what Jason did to you."

"I understand, Kristian. I truly do. I am just afraid that it will confuse her, and she won't know how to handle her emotions from a young child because of all this confusion. Veronica has you. You've been a father figure since the day she was born. She also has Janice and my parents. Can't that be enough?"

I hoped that Kristian understood where I was coming from. I didn't want to put Veronica in that position, especially because she thinks Kristian is her dad. I'm glad she has a father figure like Kristian in her life. However, I didn't want to take that away from her by forgiving Jason and potentially allowing him to come back into our lives on Veronica's behalf. Once I explained that to Kristian, his response made me see the situation more clearly.

Kristian explained that I wouldn't be forgiving Jason to allow him back into our lives. I would be forgiving Jason to allow my heart and mind to move on with life. I don't have to talk to Jason ever again to forgive him, and I don't have to let him in Veronica's life right now. If that was something she wanted to talk about down the line, then we'd handle that when the time came. For now, forgive, and move on.

After Kristian and I finished our conversation, he walked over to the crib and lay Veronica down. He then turned to me and held out his hand. I stood up, walked over to him, and held his hand. Then, he reached out his other hand, rested it on Veronica softly, and began praying over us all. He prayed for strength, clarity, good health, and peace. From that moment, I knew he was the one I wanted to marry.

13

W hen I turned seventeen and was doing good in school, I was offered a job at our church's nursery. I could bring Veronica with me and work every Wednesday, Sunday, and occasionally on Saturdays if any classes or events were being held. I was beyond grateful to have a job and I'd be able to graduate early due to my academic excellence.

I still had to rely on Kristian or my parents for transportation. I knew they didn't mind, but I felt guilty because they'd always done everything for me, and I'd only been working for a few months. I hadn't made enough to buy my own car yet, much less get my license. So I asked Kristian if he would take me to the DMV to take my written and driving test and give me driving lessons. He was all for it, and I was excited. I would finally not have to depend on everyone to help me and give them a break. I appreciated everything they did for me, but I knew after a while, it got tiring. I wanted to be able to take that stress off of them.

I downloaded the driver's handbook, and I studied for weeks. When the day finally came, I felt overly confident. Kristian drove me to the DMV, and I walked in and got signed in to take the test. When I finished the written test, I walked over to the woman at the desk and waited for a response to know if I had passed. I sat back down, patiently waiting, and looked at my phone. A text from Kristian read. *You got this. Praying for a passing grade.* I smiled and heard my name called. I inhaled deeply and walked over to the woman sitting at the desk. There was a short pause, and then she spoke.

"Congratulations, you've passed the written test. Would you like to take the driving test today or schedule it for another time?"

"If I could take it today, that would be great."

The woman nodded and handed me a paper slip, and instructed me to wait in a line at the other side of the room. Three other people were standing there waiting to take their driving test. While waiting, I texted Kristian and told him I had passed the written test and was waiting to take the driving test. I also asked him to change and feed Veronica for me when she woke up from her nap in the back seat.

When my name was finally called, a nervous feeling came over me. I got another text from Kristian telling me to put my seatbelt on before starting the engine. He never ceased to amaze me with how he would tell me things at the perfect time. I turned my phone on silent and walked out to the student driver's car. The driving instructor introduced himself and explained what I was to do. I was to drive a specific route he instructed, and then I'd have to parallel park between two traffic cones.

Once we got in the car, I immediately put my purse in the backseat and put on my seatbelt. Then I started the engine. The instructor instructed me to drive through the route, and I began the test. I followed all of the instructions perfectly. The instructor complimented me a few times, and then it came time to parallel park the car. I took a deep breath and said a quick prayer. I pulled up to the spot and backed in carefully. Unfortunately, I wasn't careful enough because I slightly tapped the cone when I backed into the space. I was worried I would fail the test, but gratefully the instructor was nice enough to not knock off any points and passed me.

I got out of the car, walked back into the DMV, and handed the woman at the desk a slip to receive my temporary license. The woman explained that obtaining the license in the mail would take seven to ten business days. So I took my temporary license and walked out of the DMV and up to Kristian's car waving it in the air. He got out of the car and hugged me tightly, congratulating me.

"I'm so relieved that I finally got my license, so now I don't have to ask my mom to take me to school so early in the morning."

Once Kristian and I got home, we walked into the house to tell my parents the good news. When I walked past the foyer, my parents stood in the living room with David. Kristian looked at everyone and then looked at me. He leaned in and whispered,

"Forgiveness applies in this situation also."

He took Veronica to her room and began getting her changed and ready to eat. I stepped into the living room and looked at my parents and David.

"What's going on?"

My parents both stood up and asked that we all had a conversation. David was here to make amends and apologize for all he'd done to me and my mom.

Remembering what Kristian said, I agreed to talk and listen. David started first and explained that he'd regretted his behavior when I was younger. Then, he asked if he would be able to spend more time with me and meet his granddaughter. I wasn't sure how I felt about anyone meeting Veronica. I was an overprotective mother, attempting to shield her from any ill intentions, whether from David, Jason, or anyone else who came into our lives. Sometimes I wish my mother had done that for me. But when I thought about my life now, that would mean I wouldn't have Veronica, and I would have never met Kristian, Janice, or my parents. David did seem genuine. He came up with a solution to prove to us that he was not drinking anymore, and he offered to take a test whenever we asked.

David truly just wanted to make up for lost time with Veronica and me, even if it was supervised. He didn't seem to care. So I decided to forgive him and work towards rebuilding our relationship. But before that, I had one request from him.

"If you want to work on rebuilding our relationship, then I want you to consistently start attending church service with us."

I wanted my dad to prioritize God in his life, and if he agreed, things could work. But I needed to see him put in the effort first. He'd never been the type to go to church, so this would be a big step for him, and if he goes consistently, then it would prove to me that his intentions are good.

In the following weeks, I was surprised that David kept his word about attending church service. He only missed one week due to having started a new job. He told me later that he requested that he take Sundays off to allow him to go to church weekly. I was proud of him for putting in the time and effort to show that he was serious about making up lost time. I appreciated his effort. I hadn't felt comfortable letting Veronica around him until I knew his intentions, but I continued praying about it.

Two months later, Kristian and I discussed the next steps in getting closer with David. He told me he was proud of me for my willingness to forgive and the effort I'd put in to allow David to be in my life. During our conversation, I explained that I decided the time was right and allowed David to officially meet and spend time with Veronica and me. It would be a supervised visit but, that was me showing that I was attempting to allow things to move forward with David. Kristian agreed and offered to let me use his car to meet David, so I didn't have to worry about David picking me up.

The following day I texted David and told him if he was able and interested, I would allow him to meet Veronica, and we could go out for the day. He responded quickly.

"Rose, I'm so happy you have allowed me to meet Veronica and spend time with you both. I'm off on Saturday. Would that work for you?"

"Yes, Saturday sounds good. Can we meet at Dobbins Park at 11 A.M.?"

"Sounds great. I'll see you then."

I was nervous about meeting him with Veronica alone. Still, I gave Kristian and my parents all the information so everyone knew where I'd be if anything went downhill.

Saturday came, and I got Veronica dressed and her bag packed with all the essentials. I texted David to confirm we were still going to meet, and Kristian picked us up around 10 A.M. He drove us back to his house to drop him off, then I drove off toward the park. I saw David standing under the pavilion with a gift bag when we arrived. I unbuckled Veronica from her car seat, grabbed her diaper bag from the floorboard, closed and locked the car, and walked over to David.

14

When Veronica and I approached David, he smiled and held out a gift bag for Veronica. Skeptical, I peeked inside the bag and found some toddler toys, feeding utensils, and a pack of sippy cups. I walked over to the grass and allowed Veronica to open the bag herself and explore the contents. David then handed me an envelope that had my name written on it.

"Before you open this, I just want to tell you again how sorry I am for everything that took place between your mother and me. I was struggling with addiction and felt lost and

disconnected from reality. This is not to try to win you back. I will understand if you don't want it, but I'll also understand if you take it and never speak to me again. I just thought I could try to do something to help you now, even though it took seventeen years."

After David's confession and heartfelt apology, I hesitated to open the envelope. I didn't know what I was going to find. Once I did, there was a picture of my parents and me at the same park when I was a few months old. Everyone in the picture looked happy. I became confused because I thought I was the reason their marriage had gone down the drain. Come to find out, David explained that my mother had an affair around the time she had gotten pregnant. David had never truly known if I was his biological child or not. He felt distant toward me but tried not to allow that to get the best of him. My mother then had another affair after I was born, which led to David's alcoholism and abusive behavior.

Once he left, he attempted to get clean with a fresh start in a different part of town. David then pointed to the envelope so I could continue to pull out what remained inside.

There was a check for $2,000 and a car key. Unsure, I asked David for clarity as I held up the key and the check. He explained that he had been working to help save up for a car for himself, so he didn't have to take the bi-state bus, but with my current situation, he wanted to give me the car. If for some reason, I didn't want the car, there was a check to use for a down payment for something different.

I was appalled by David's version of events that took place. I almost didn't believe it. Rebecca left out so many details of the events that David told me. When I told David what Rebecca told me and what happened after he left, he was so disgusted that he started crying. He genuinely felt bad for me. Whether I was biologically his or not, a child should have never endured the emotional pain and trauma that I did. He couldn't stop apologizing. I expressed my feelings on the situation and was glad things worked out the way they did.

After the meet with David at the park, things got much better in our relationship. Sarah and Robert were happy that he had made the necessary changes to be a part of Veronica and my life for the better. I was also glad to have David back. Since David told me he wasn't sure if I was biologically his daughter, I talked to Sarah and Robert about wanting to go through with a DNA test. They helped me get the kit, and David and I set up a time to do a mouth swab to send the kit off.

Thirty-three days later, Kristian came into the house with the mail. The results were in, and I called David immediately. That evening, David came over while my parents sat in the living room, ready to read the results per David and my request. David was nervous, and his nervousness made me hesitant and scared as well. We walked into the dining room, sat at the table, and waited for Robert to open the envelope. Robert put on his reading glasses and cleared his throat. He was quiet for a few minutes, reading through all the information on the paperwork, and then he looked at David and me. I took a deep breath and felt Kristian's hand on my shoulder, somewhat easing my anxiety.

"Well, David, it states here that you're 99.99% Rose's biological father."

Knowing that David was my biological father lifted a massive weight off his chest. He burst into tears and took my hand. He looked at me and apologized again. I was happy to know that David was my biological father, not some unknown man I'd lived with during my childhood. Kristian took that cue to walk over to David and initiate a conversation. They walked out of the back door while I tended to Veronica when she woke up from her nap. I had no idea what was coming next.

Kristian then surprised everyone by walking in from the kitchen with a bottle of wine. Soon after, Janice walked through the front door. Kristian smiled, then poured a glass of wine for the adults and some sparkling apple-cranberry juice for him and I. Kristian knew I loved sparkling juice, so he always kept a big bottle on hand. What came next was astounding.

While talking with the other women, I heard my name called. I turned around to Kristian down on one knee with a ring box showing a beautiful diamond ring. I couldn't speak.

"Rose, from the moment I met you, I knew you would be the one. We have both walked a rough path, and we promised each other that we stick together no matter what happens. Allowing us to work together to better

ourselves, our future, and Veronica's. So, will you marry me, Rose?"

Tears of joy fell from my eyes. I was so lucky to have Kristian in my life. He was the man of my dreams. He was the best father I could ask for for my daughter, even though she wasn't his biological child. She loved him as he was, and so did he. He treated me the way I deserved to be treated, and he made sure to keep us protected. He was a devoted gentleman with a pure heart, and I couldn't have asked for anything better in a man and a loving father.

15

On the morning of May twelfth, I got up and got myself and Veronica ready. My parents, David, Kristian, Janice, and Olivia were all at my parent's house scrambling to get prepared for the big day. Finally, I walked across the stage to receive my high school diploma. I was so proud of myself for pushing myself to make it where I was. I was thankful to Kristian and my entire family for supporting me. I did it, allowing me to finish high school even with a baby on my hip!

As I walked across the stage when my name was called, I watched and heard my family applaud me. The principal even allowed Veronica to walk with me on the stage to receive my diploma. The support I was given throughout my high school years with Veronica was substantial. I made a difference in many lives, but the impact that so many people have made on mine was especially significant. I couldn't be more thankful.

After high school, I didn't want to take a break, knowing I had such a great support system. I wanted to sign up at the local college to receive my Master's in psychology. But Kristian explained that it would be easier if we had gotten married first so I wouldn't have to go through the trouble with my name change. So we decided to have a small wedding before I officially started school again. The next evening, we decided to get everyone together and tell them our plans so Robert could schedule our wedding at the church.

I wasn't big on all the fancy weddings. I wanted something simple and heartfelt and the people who mattered the most to be there. We were lucky to have a space on the schedule at the end of June. That was perfect. We had time to get my dress and Kristian's tuxedo and make the necessary arrangements. Janice handled the cake, and David helped purchase some of the decorations.

My mom and Janice took me to try on a few dresses, and Robert and David took Kristian to get fitted for a tux. There were so many beautiful dresses when we got to the bridal shop. I looked for about an hour and found something that was beautiful. I decided to try it on but realized no price tag was attached to it. So I asked the bridal stylist about the price, and she took it to her manager to ask.

When she came back, she told me the dress was $6,400. My jaw dropped.

"I think I should put that back and look for something different."

My mom walked in as I asked to put the dress back and asked,

"Put what back?"
"I was going to put this dress back and look for something more affordable. The price just seems too steep."

My mom asked to see the price tag, and I showed it to her. She looked at me and then again at the dress.

"Let's put it on the rack to try on and look at a few different choices at once."

I agreed, put the dress on the rack, and continued looking for more dresses. We searched for another hour and found a total of five dresses that I liked. Now it was time to try them all on and choose which one was the best.

I tried on one dress after the next, and while I tried on the last dress, my mom found a dress hanging in the corner behind a mannequin. She pulled it out and hung it on the rack for me to try. I stepped up in front of the mirror when I walked out of the fitting room. I looked at myself intently in the dress and then turned around to look at my mom and Janice, not for their approval but more so for their denial. I hate that dress, and I wanted to rip it off. My mom and Janice both winced at the sight of the dress. It looked like an oversized nightgown.

My mom stated as she handed me the hanger and sat back down,

"Good thing I found this over there. Why don't you try it on, Rose?"

I took the dress and walked into the fitting room to try it on. Ten minutes later, I walked out wearing the biggest smile. I loved how the dress fit me. I stepped in front of the mirror and turned to look at my mom and Janice, who were in awe at how beautiful that dress was on me. Six dresses down, and almost five hours later, I found the dress. It was slightly over my budget, but we made it work.

Once we left the bridal shop, Janice called Kristian to see how their luck was finding a nice tuxedo. They had made the purchase two hours prior and were waiting for us to finish up. My dad insisted on taking us all out to dinner since no one would be in the mood to cook when we got home. I was grateful for that because I was absolutely starving.

We neatly tucked the dress in the car's trunk, got in, and left to meet the guys at the restaurant. When we finally arrived, we all stepped out of the car and walked inside to be seated. It was nice to have my biological dad back in the picture. But, to be surrounded by all the loving and supportive people in my life, I was beyond grateful. We all shared laughs, memories, and funny moments with Veronica for the rest of the night.

The rest of the month flew by. David was involved consistently in Veronica's and my life, and Kristian also formed a bond with David. I was most appreciative that David respected my adoptive parents, Robert and Sarah. Occasionally, I thought about Rebecca and if she would've been genuinely proud of me. It hurt my heart to know if what David said was true about Rebecca. I didn't want to believe it, but Rebecca had changed so much over the years, and now that she's gone, I'll never know the truth. I didn't know how hard it would be to let something like that go. I could forgive, but forgiveness wasn't the problem. The problem was understanding the truth about what happened and why. I felt like I had a right to now.

June twenty-seventh finally rolled around, and it was Kristian's and my big day. We were getting married. I was so grateful that God allowed us to cross paths the way we did. We agreed to do couples counseling so we knew how to address the things of our past and not use that against one another during our marriage. Kristian was always the patient and understanding one. I had a hard time learning how to be patient, especially if it caused me anxiety.

The wedding was beautiful, from the venue to the small decorations The five-tier cake was amazing, and our family surrounded us with the utmost respect and support. All of my life, I never thought I'd get married. From my past experiences to childhood trauma, I never thought I'd find someone who'd be willing to genuinely love me and want me as their wife. Although I was no longer a virgin and had a baby out of wedlock, Kristian didn't once condemn me for it. Instead, he stepped up and helped me to see what an amazing woman I was despite everything I had been through.

16

Two months after the wedding, I finally decided to sign up for school. After I had signed up, I had to wait almost six months for my transcripts and financial aid to kick in. I made the decision to get my Bachelor's degree in psychology. I wanted to take part-time classes instead of full-time because I wanted to have time at home to spend with Kristian and Veronica. During that time, Kristian and I bought our first home. Veronica and Kristian decided to not include me in a new addition to the family when I got home from work one evening.

I walked into the front door, only to step on a squeaker toy and a soiled puppy pad. Then, already somewhat ticked off that Kristian didn't come to me first, I walked into the dining room to find a giant dog crate with Kristian locked inside.

"That look suits you."

I stated as I walked into the room, setting my bags down.

"What are you doing in there, and where is Veronica?"
"Veronica is the one who locked me in here and ran off with the pup."

I couldn't help but laugh even though I wasn't happy because he didn't consult me about getting a dog.

When I helped Kristian out of the dog crate, I yelled out to Veronica, and the next thing I knew, I had a giant barreling through my hallway, right towards me. Bracing for the impact, I leaned towards the wall waiting for the dog and me to collide and hit the floor. Once that finally happened, I was attacked by sloppy, playful kisses. I finally got my bearings and stood up, looking at Kristian with a straight face.

"It's one thing to not talk to me about getting a puppy, but to not talk to me about getting a fifty pound, four-month-old great dane puppy?!"

Kristian, smirked, and shrugged his shoulders. If I'm going to be honest, the puppy was undeniably cute. Veronica ran over, gave me the biggest hug, and asked,

"Mommy, what are we going to name him?"
"Well, baby, what do you think? Will you name him something by his markings or personality?"

Veronica had grown so much. She was very creative and loved animals. My parents had a dog that Veronica had a close bond with. When I was pregnant, their dog Sadie was stuck to my hip. When Veronica was a baby, Sadie used to lay her head on Veronica's bouncer and snuggle with her tiny feet. I later discovered that the puppy we had adopted came from the same breeder that Sadie did.

"Jax!"

Veronica shouted from her bedroom. Well, it was fitting. Jax was all black with a white splatter spot on him that looked similar to the game piece. I chuckled and yelled back down the hall,

"Very fitting!"

Jax fit in with the family perfectly. We still had some training to work on with him, but he quickly caught on. He had a loving personality, and Jax and Veronica were inseparable. I loved the bond they formed from the beginning.

Three months later, Jax had grown so much. He'd become overly clingy, especially when Veronica was at school. I didn't know what had changed in him. He would bounce back and forth between Veronica and me consistently. So when I brought it up to

Kristian, he told me he had some indication as to why Jax was stuck to my hip.
Kristian explained that the reason Jax was following me around constantly was because he thought that maybe I was pregnant. He then reminded me of how Sadie followed me around the same way. My eyes immediately widened, and my jaw dropped.

"Oh my gosh, Kristian!"

I shouted playfully until I realized I hadn't had my period that month. I stopped, turned to look at the giant wall calendar, and looked back at Kristian, who looked at me intently.

"You should probably take a test."

Baffled at the current dilemma I had on my hands, I dropped everything and ran out of the house. I got into the car and drove straight to the market a few blocks down the road. When I arrived, I pulled into the first parking space I saw and darted into the store. I ran down the isles looking for the pregnancy tests, and when I found them, I grabbed three. *Just to be safe.* I thought to myself.

I walked up to the registers to check out, and my hands began to tremble when I looked up and noticed that Jason was the cashier. He looked at me and smirked once he saw what I was buying.

"I see you got married."

Jason's remarks made me feel highly uncomfortable. But I remembered what Kristian said about forgiving him. As much as I hated that, I knew it was right.

Jason rang up my three pregnancy tests and told me my total. I pulled out my bank card and paid. I started to walk away, but I stopped, prayed to God for strength, turned back around, and said,

"Jason, even after everything you put me through, just know that I forgive you."

I took a deep breath and let out a massive sigh of relief. I walked out of the store, leaving Jason stunned. In my mind, I made a note to never go to that store again. The frustration from thinking about the past with Jason got to me, but I forgave, and now I will have to force myself to forget.

While thinking about how well I handled that encounter with Jason, I completely forgot why I went to the store in the first place. I jumped into the car, started the engine, and drove home. I ran inside and told Kristian about how I ran into Jason, and I took his advice on forgiving him. Kristian was proud of me, and I was proud of myself. Something I thought I could never do, I finally did.

I put the bag on the counter and grabbed a water bottle from the fridge. I chugged it down in hopes I would have to use the bathroom soon. Soon after, I finally had to go. I grabbed a test and walked into the bathroom. I took the test, and I started to become nervous. I asked myself if I was ready for this. My body had gone through so much trauma getting pregnant at such a young age.

I washed my hands and waited for the test results to show. A piece of me hoped I was. I would've loved to have a child with Kristian. I knew he would be a great father after practically helping to raise Veronica. I waited for the results to show what would significantly impact our lives and family in such a way.

Unfortunately, the results showed negative. I wasn't pregnant. I became somewhat depressed because I hoped I was.

I walked out of the bathroom, trying to hold back tears, when I saw Kristian staring at me. I shook my head no at him, and the tears I tried to keep in came flowing out. I couldn't control my emotions. Kristian wrapped his arms around me and hugged me tight.

"I love you. It may just not be time yet. It'll happen. We just have to trust God's plan."

Kristian always knew how to make me feel better.

17

It had been a month since I had taken the pregnancy test. I kept remembering what Kristian said about trusting God's plan and timing. I thought about how I needed to pray more and thank God for allowing me to see another day. I had a rough walk in life from an early age. So it was time that I thanked God. I walked into my bedroom, kneeled on the side of the bed, and prayed.

"Lord, thank you for saving me. Thank you for allowing me to be placed with a family

who genuinely loved and cared about Veronica and me. Thank you for allowing Kristian to cross my path. I love him with all my heart and soul, Lord. We want another child. I ask that you bless us both with a child to add to our family. In your name, we pray, Amen."

A month later, I started realizing little things here and there that were completely out of the norm for me. My face started breaking out, I started having weird cravings, and I couldn't stop running to the bathroom. Jax was acting even more strange, and Veronica was clinging to my side. She would insist on sleeping with me every night. Veronica was not the social type of butterfly like her mother. In fact, she was the complete opposite. Something was off for her to be as clingy to me as she was.

That night Kristian had to work a little later than usual. I finally got Veronica to sleep in her own bed. While I had some quiet time, I decided to take a bubble bath. I walked into the bathroom, grabbed a bath towel from the closet, and noticed the two pregnancy tests still sitting on the shelf. I looked in the mirror at my face, then glanced back to the shelf. I grabbed the test, opened the package, and set up the contents on the counter. I took the test and expected to wait the allotted time stated in the directions.

Almost immediately, two dark lines showed up on the screen. Initially, I thought I was seeing things and thought it was wrong. So I grabbed the other test and took that one too. Now I had two pregnancy tests on the counter that showed very positive.

"Thank you, God! You allowed me to carry another child." I said loudly.

I then showered, cleaned myself up, and got out and dressed. By that time, Kristian had walked through the front door.

I walked out of the bathroom and up to Kristian and hugged him.

"I have to show you something."

I took him by the hand and walked him into the bathroom to show him the two gifts I had left on the counter for him. He looked closely and then looked at me intently.

"Are you pregnant?"

"Yes!"

I tried to contain my excitement and not scream, potentially waking up Veronica and Jax.

The next day Kristian and I called over our families to share the news. When they arrived, no one knew what the news was about. Kristian stood up and said,

"We called you to share some amazing news we just recently found out."

He reached his hand out for me to stand next to him. I picked up Veronica, and we shared the news of my pregnancy. Everyone jumped out of their seats and ran up to Kristian and I. Veronica shouted and clapped her hands, making me smile.

Later when I thought about it, it made sense that Jax and Veronica had become clingy. I'd heard about that before, and it didn't bother me one bit. I loved them, and I was glad they had gotten closer, and my pregnancy didn't drive us apart. During the midst of sharing our news, I received a phone call. I quickly handed Veronica to my mom and ran into the other room.

I answered the phone, and on the other end was an admissions counselor from Columbia University. One of the top colleges for the psychology program. They explained that the local college in the city I signed for initially sent them my transcripts and stated that Columbia University would love it if I came into the admissions office to take a tour if I chose to attend their school. I was speechless. I agreed, set up a time and day to meet with the admissions counselor, and hung up the phone.

When I walked back into the living room, I got everyone's attention and explained the other news I had to share. Everyone was shouting and praising, and I just stood there thinking about how truly blessed I was. To be wanted by the best college in New York City for psychology was a blessing in itself, but to be pregnant, too; I had a lot to be thankful for. All I had to worry about was how I was going to attend college while I was pregnant.

I knew it would be a lot on my body, but I was confident in myself and put my trust in God that I would be okay. I scheduled an appointment with the University next week to take a tour and talk with the admissions counselor. I prayed that they would be understanding of my pregnancy and would allow me to take the necessary time off when the time came. I grabbed a notebook and decided to jot down all of my notes and questions to ask them when I arrived for the meeting.

The next morning Kristian walked into the kitchen, let Jax outside, and poured a cup of coffee. He turned to me and took my hand, and kissed it.

"I'm very proud of you, Rose. You're a great mother and wife, and you will be a great counselor."

"Thank you, Kristian. I love you and appreciate your support."

I stood up from the barstool and wrapped my arms around my husband. I was beyond grateful for my family and the opportunity to be wanted by the top University in the city.

Later that day, I had a list of things I had to get done and phone calls to make. The first thing I did was called and made an appointment at the doctor's office about my pregnancy. When I called, I was surprised that they could get me in the same day due to a couple cancellations. So I ran over to the calendar to see which time would work best for me and scheduled it.

Kristian left to take Veronica and Jax for a walk. I called his cell and explained that I could get in with the obstetrician the same day. He was able to make arrangements with his job, and my parents would keep Veronica while we were at the doctor's office. When it was time to go, we dropped Veronica off at my parents and drove to the clinic. When we arrived, I got checked in and sat down next to Kristian, waiting to be called back.

My name was finally called twenty minutes later, and we walked back into a room. I was instructed to give a urine sample and, when I was done, to lay on the table. I waited for the doctor to come in and check the baby's heartbeat and do an ultrasound. Once we heard the baby's heartbeat, Kristian wept softly. The doctor seemed to think I was further along than we initially thought and decided to do an ultrasound and blood work to determine the gestation age.

Once we saw the ultrasound, our little bundle of joy was much bigger than it should've been this early on in my pregnancy. It was only a month prior that I took a test that showed negative. But from the ultrasound, the baby was measured at around nine weeks gestation. This took me by surprise. I wasn't sure how it was possible to be further along when I only found out the night before. I just knew I was happy as long as the baby was healthy.

18

It had been a week since Kristian and I had been to the doctor. My pregnancy was going well, and I had little morning sickness. I was grateful. I got ready for the meeting at the University. Then I kissed Kristian and Veronica goodbye and walked out of the house. I drove to the school, parked, and confidently walked inside the main office. I requested to speak with the admissions counselor, and soon after, I walked in for my meeting.

I reviewed several things during the meeting, including tuition and my pregnancy. With the information I was given, I decided to sign up. I was moved over to a different counselor named Clarissa. She helped me with my schedule and all the classes I would need to take, and I was also offered a full-ride scholarship. On top of that, I was given four months to take my classes from home when it was time for me to deliver the baby.

After leaving the school, I stopped by a donut shop and a produce stand to get something to eat. I had started having some weird cravings that, in all honesty, sounded disgusting. Glazed donut holes and cherry tomatoes. I didn't remember having such sickening cravings with Veronica. But, on a side note, my face was clear, and my skin was glowing. I could get used to this look.

Once I got home, I walked inside to Kristian cooking dinner and Veronica sneaking meatloaf to Jax under the table. I kissed them both, took my plate from Kristian, and sat down. Kristian asked,

"How did it go?"

"It went very well. I decided to sign up and was set up with a counselor, and when we went over tuition, the counselor said I was approved for a full-ride scholarship. But the best part is that I was given four months to take my courses at home when I'd be out for maternity leave."

"Rose, that is amazing! I'm so proud of you."

"God is amazing! He never fails to bless us abundantly.

"That he is."

The next few weeks were a breeze. I started my classes at Columbia University and decided to take full-time courses. I could still be home on time for dinner, and I had the weekends off to allot for church and extra time to spend with Veronica, Kristian, and Jax. It was a change that Veronica had to get used to, but every weekend, I made it up to her by going to the park, taking nature hikes, and playtime at my parent's house.

My five-month visit with the obstetrician's office came up fast. I left school early to make my appointment, and Kristian met me there. We walked in, I got checked in, and we waited until I was called back. Once I was called, we walked back to the room, and I got ready for my ultrasound. This was the day we'd find out what I was having. Kristian and I were both hoping for a boy. The time had come, and the ultrasound technician came in and began the ultrasound. I watched closely at the ultrasound monitor as the technician glided the wand across my stomach.

"Do you want to know the gender of the baby?"

I nodded excitedly at the technician's question. She kept moving the wand around and asked me to move in a few different positions to get a better look. The technician snapped an ultrasound picture and then wrote on the screen; *IT'S A BOY!* She then got a good view of his face and printed them out for us.

Kristian and I both walked out of the office with big smiles. Once we got in the car, I texted everyone to tell them the news that we were having a boy. On the ride home, Kristian and I talked about baby boy names. We went over a few that neither of us could both agree on. Later that night, as we were getting in bed,

Kristian stopped in the doorway and looked at me.

"What about Jesiah?"
"Oh, I like that, and it's biblical."
"It means The Lord Exists."
"Well, I can't argue with that one."

I laughed. We both agreed, and I sent a quick text telling everyone the name we picked for our little man.

The next few months got harder on me the bigger my stomach grew. I had a much harder time walking from class to class around the University. It had gotten so bad that the doctor suggested I continue my studies from home if possible because I had so much swelling that I could potentially be considered high-risk. I knew I didn't want that, so I requested that I move to remote classes per my doctor's request. The school was able to approve my request, and I was able to bring all of my schoolwork home and work remotely.

Veronica was happy with the new change, even though she didn't quite understand that I had to focus on my work so I could be an effective counselor. I knew I would be great at it. I had a vision that I wanted to open my own office to be a trauma counselor. I was sure I wanted to help children and adults placed in the foster system at any time in their lives.

By the time I was halfway through my first year of school, Jesiah had made an unexpected grand entrance. I was in the grocery store with Veronica getting a few things, and suddenly my water broke. Jesiah caused a scene and got the attention of several people in the store, including a paramedic on break. I instantly called Kristian and let him know what was going on. The paramedic called it in and loaded Veronica and me into the ambulance.

"Call the rest of the family, please, and meet us at the hospital."
"Okay, I'm on my way. I love you."

Kristian sounded nervous on the phone with me. I don't know if it was because we didn't know how far dilated I was or because Veronica was with us, and we didn't want to traumatize her at such a young age. Obviously, that wouldn't be something we would plan to do, but considering the circumstances, we did what we had to do. We made it to the hospital within fifteen minutes. My contractions were getting stronger and closer together.

As soon as they got me into a room, my parents, Kristian and Janice, ran into the room to check on Veronica and me. Janice took Veronica to the waiting room with my dad as my labor progressed. My mom and Kristian stayed with me during labor and delivery. I could tell it would be a quick process since things advanced so quickly to begin with. Then, with only a few short pushes, Jesiah made his grand entrance.

After Jesiah was born, we stayed in the hospital for a few days and were discharged home. Things got back to normal quickly. I was back in school, taking my courses online. Once I got through the third semester, the school emailed me requesting to put me in advanced classes since I had mastered all my freshman college courses. Surprisingly, as tired as I was after having Jesiah, not getting much sleep, and breastfeeding every few hours, I felt drained. But I still managed to keep my grades up and moved to advanced classes.

EPILOGUE
Three Years Later

The next few years flew by. Jesiah was three years old, and Veronica was seven years old. Kristian finished his classes and became the head youth pastor at New Life Church. Finally, I was ready to walk across the stage to receive my Bachelor's degree in Psychology. I had a deja-vu moment thinking about how I walked across the stage when I graduated high school. Then, with Veronica on my hip, I walked across the stage. The only difference, I had Sophia, our newest addition.

Sophia was born eight months before I graduated from the University. It took me a little longer because I had some complications with her at the end of my pregnancy. I had to have an emergency cesarean section because her umbilical cord was wrapped around her neck, and she was in the breech position. After I brought her home, I managed through the pain from my incision and continued my coursework, and I graduated with honors.

Once it came time for me to take what I learned into the real world, I reached out to Janice. While I was still in the foster system, Janice left the group home and opened her own facility. In that facility, there was access to free counseling services. That's where I came in. I counseled children from the ages of five to eighteen. I also counseled adults who spent fourteen days or longer in the foster system. Knowing how traumatizing the foster system was, I wanted to offer a shorter time frame for people who were placed in the system. All I requested was their file; I reviewed their background and would help them in any way possible to receive the services they deserved.

In the process, I also passed along information to the teens and adults if they wanted to visit New Life Church. When they came back to see me, they would thank me for allowing them to open another door in their lives. All I asked was that they spread their experience of the gift of getting saved to others. Kristian led the youth down the path to righteousness and helped some of those struggling see a new light, giving them a sense of purpose within the church. They had the ability to create something that mattered to them. That was what meant the most to Kristian and me.

The pain that you've been feeling, can't compare to the joy that's coming.

Romans 8:18